BOOKS BY JOAB STIEGLITZ

The Utgarda Trilogy

The Old Man's Request

The Missing Medium

The Other Realm

The Thule Trilogy

The Hunter in the Shadows:

The Missing Medium

Book Two of the Utgarda Series

Joab Stieglitz

ISBN: 978-1-7332047-2-9

Published in the United States by Rantings of a Wandering Mind

In memory of Steve Russell, without whose expertise, assistance, and encouragement this book would never have been published.

DEDICATION

This book is dedicated to my wife, without whose continual support and relentless encouragement it may never have been finished.

ACKNOWLEDGMENTS

I would like to acknowledge all the people who inspired, encouraged, assisted, and supported me through this effort.

Many thanks to Steph, Blake, Viv, Sam, Liz, Mike, Greg, Jenna, Dave and Josiah for wading through my drafts and proposing, or demanding, edits, changes, and other suggestions.

Thanks to the Springfield Writers group for listening, critiquing, and suggesting things that made the story all the better, especially Susan, John, Fred, Duane, and Carol.

Chapter 1

July 9, 1929

Doctor Harold Lamb was exhausted. In the three weeks since the incident at the farm in Stuckley where he, the anthropologist Anna Rykov, and Father Sean O'Malley had banished the malevolent entity Utgarda, he had been interrogated by the police and hounded by reporters almost constantly.

"It looks like you have been exonerated," Eliezer Feldman said, looking at the morning edition of the *Sullivan Observer*. "The inquest has ruled Wilson's death as a suicide."

The apparent suicide of Wilson Longborough, only son of the late Reister University trustee and philanthropist Jason Longborough, was big news in the sleepy, college town of Wellersburg. In reality, Wilson Longborough had been an embodiment of Utgarda and had disappeared when the ritual was completed.

"Is there any mention of Cophen?" Lamb asked. The detective hired to help them had been possessed by Utgarda some time before the whole series of events had begun. Cophen's existence was not widely known, so the doctor, the anthropologist, and the priest had put the corpse in Wilson's car and used it to start the conflagration that reduced the farmhouse to ash.

"Nothing is mentioned here," Feldman said, scanning the article again.

"That is a relief," Anna Rykov sighed. "It will be good to get into my own bed again." Like Lamb, the Russian-born anthropologist had been the guest of Feldman, the director of the Reister University library since the news first came out.

"Then that should put an end to the Cabal's experimentation with the occult," Lamb said with finality. Jason Longborough and his friends had innocently set the chain of events in motion fifty years ago. By June 1929, Longborough had been the last survivor of the group that had called itself the Cabal.

"There are still a lot of unanswered questions," Feldman said. The Director of the Reister University Library had been given the responsibility of dealing with the strange happenings that had occurred in and around Reister University almost since its founding, and a trust fund to finance the response to such activities.

"How did Jason know that he would need your assistance?" Feldman queried. Longborough had assembled Rykov, Lamb, and O'Malley; an expert in early Russian culture, a scientist, and a clergyman, who Longborough had assessed as all being willing to participate in the quest.

"He also went to great lengths to provide what you would need," Feldman added. Longborough had ensured that the ancient tomes required for the ritual had been maintained and preserved as part of the university library's collection. He had brought the Exotic Spice and Tea Shop, an Oriental sorcerer's workshop, to Wellersburg so that the unique materials that they would require were available. And he had retained ownership of the lonely farm in Stuckley where the original ritual had taken place.

"For that matter, how and when did Utgarda possess Wilson?" Lamb said.

"And what about Arthur Cophen?" Anna added.

"Cophen was apparently under Utgarda's power before he came to Wellersburg," Feldman conceded. The librarian had hired Cophen to assist Longborough's team in completing the ritual. "And even though he ultimately turned on you, his death seems to have been the final, critical component in banishing Utgarda."

"Perhaps things can return to normal again," Lamb said, but his tone belied his doubt. Like Rykov, the doctor had been virtually imprisoned in Feldman's house outside Wellersburg to avoid the relentless hounding by the press. The doctor and the anthropologist had both been suspended from their posts at the University pending the outcome of the investigation. Their own homes had been staked out by reporters night and day since the news broke. Only Father O'Malley had seemed to escape the spectacle. He had been summoned to meet with his superiors and had left Wellersburg the day after the events in Stuckley had taken place.

"I don't think that is possible," Anna said gravely, absently running her fingers over the scabs where she had been attacked by an extradimensional monster. "Cophen warned us that we could not stop once we went down this path." Feldman agreed.

"Like it or not," the librarian added, "you have been exposed to things beyond the knowledge or reason of most. And they have been exposed to you." He put a supportive hand on Lamb's shoulder. "I have seen many a good man changed by these phenomena. Sometimes, they were not even aware of it."

"Like Cophen," Lamb said. Feldman nodded.

"And even if you can return to your normal life," Feldman said grimly, "the experience will stay with you."

"I received a postcard from Sean," Anna said, breaking the awkward silence. "It is from Rome." Her eyebrows peaked conspiratorially. "It says that the SS Conte Grande from Naples will arrive in New York at Pier 39 on 13th of July."

"So he was summoned to Rome," the librarian said with interest. Then his expression changed. "I don't think much will happen over the next few days. Why don't you and Dr. Lamb meet his ship when it arrives?"

"It would be good to get away from here," Lamb said. "No offense, sir, but your home has become rather confining."

"I understand fully," the librarian replied with a smile. "And while you are in the city," he added, "you could run an errand for me."

"What kind of errand?" Anna asked with suspicion.

"You mentioned that Jason Longborough had spoken to Brian Teplow, the spirit medium, and that, as a consequence of that meeting, Longborough's mind had been put at ease."

"What about it?" Lamb asked with irritation.

"Well," the librarian continued, "in spite of that visit, Jason suffered a relapse of his anxieties that caused him to be hospitalized again and precipitated his calling on you to perform that ritual."

"And you wish to know what was said," Anna said matter-of-factly.

"Exactly. As you now know, his fears were not unfounded. But something the medium told him calmed his nerves." He shrugged. "It's a loose end in the story, and the official account needs to be as complete as possible." Anna and Lamb looked at each other skeptically. "It's no bother. I've been calling his agent, a Woody Frank, in order to speak to Teplow myself, but this Frank fellow is avoiding my calls." Feldman's guests still did not appear to be swayed. "The trust fund will cover all your travel and expenses, and you'll be out of the limelight for a few days. What do you say?"

"You should have been direct," Anna said with a shake of her head. "I sense there is more to the story."

"All right," the librarian said with resignation. He pulled a piece of paper from his pocket. "I asked Janice Longborough if she knew where Jason had met with Teplow. She gave me an address in Brooklyn. I sent a telegram to Brian at that address and I received this reply." He handed the slip to Anna. She read it aloud.

"Brian missing. Stop," she read. "Police have no leads. Stop. Fear the worst. Stop. Can you help? Stop. Maureen Teplow."

"Well that changes the complexion of things," Lamb said in an irritated tone. "More mystery surrounding our recent adventure." He looked to Anna. "Why would we even consider getting involved now that things are finally getting back to normal?"

"This is the missing piece of the puzzle," Anna replied. She seemed to consider things for a moment and tapped her lip with her index finger. "Utgarda is a trickster god. Banishing with a ritual does not destroy a god. It just makes it go away temporarily.

"Utgarda went to great lengths for its plan." She counted her points on her fingers. "It provided the gold box containing the amber. It inspired Brett Hanke to perform the ritual. It haunted Jason Longborough enough for him to spend his life preparing for a counter ritual. And yet, his conversation with this medium somehow threatens Utgarda's plan. Which is why he had to possess Cophen to spy on us." She paused. "There must be more to this plan."

"And things are hardly back to normal," Feldman added. "It will take time for this to blow over. You may have avoided legal complications, but the public will still view you with suspicion for a while until there is something else to occupy their attention."

"Getting away might be good for us," Anna said with an encouraging smile. "There is nothing for us here right now. A trip to Brooklyn might be just what doctor ordered!"

◆

July 11, 1929

Lamb and Rykov sat alone in a first class compartment. Under the cover of darkness, Feldman had driven the two to Albany, where they caught the overnight train to Penn Station in New York. The platform had been sparsely populated, but two suspicious characters who might have been reporters were waiting there, and Anna was afraid that they might have been recognized.

"If we were seen," Anna said, "there could be a mob of reporters waiting on the platform when we arrive."

"I don't think they saw us," Lamb replied with a confident smile. "We stayed out of sight until people got off and mixed with the crowd before boarding." Anna did not seem convinced. "Well there's nothing we can do about it. We'll just have to improvise when we get there."

"In the meantime," Anna said warily, "we should stay in the compartment until the train arrives. There are three stops before Penn Station. We do not know who might board the train between here and there."

"Very well," Lamb said with a shrug. "Unless we need the privies."

◆

The rhythm of the train through the darkness eventually lulled Lamb to sleep. Anna, however, was on edge. In spite of the late hour, there were still people moving up and down the aisle outside their compartment. A couple of times people looked in through the window in the doorway, but Anna's scowl quickly sent them on their way. Eventually, Lamb closed the blind. She could still see silhouettes as they passed by.

Anna had brought a copy of the new issue of *Science* magazine to read on the trip. Dr. Feldman maintained subscriptions to all manner of esoteric publications for the university. She had found *Immunological Prophecy from Ancient Hieroglyphics* by a Dr. W. H. Manwaring of Stanford interesting, but the other articles failed to keep her interest. She had nodded off somewhere in the middle of *A Mechanical Parallel to the Conditioned Reflex* by Professor Clark L. Hull and H. D. Baernsten.

Anna was awakened by a sudden lurch of another train that passed by in the opposite direction at speed. She glanced out the window and noticed that the passengers on the other train all had their faces pressed against the windows. Their features were distorted in expressions of anguish and they appeared to be screaming in horror, though Anna could not hear them over the noise of the trains. She nudged Lamb to wake him, but by the time the doctor opened his eyes, the other train had passed. He gave Anna a bleary-eyed look and was asleep again almost immediately. When Anna next awoke, the sun was shining between the buildings as the train passed through suburban New Jersey heading for the North River Tunnels.

Chapter 2

July 11, 1929

Shortly after 8:00 a.m., Anna and the doctor were negotiating the crowds on the main concourse. The hall was packed with hurried commuters and luggage-laden travelers. Here and there children ran through the crowds hawking newspapers. "Rome throng greets American Fliers," cried one boy over the din of the crowd, "Yancey and Williams meet with Mussolini."

"Here you go, son," Lamb said, handing the boy a coin. The child pocketed it, handed the doctor a copy of the *New York Herald*, and disappeared into the throng before Lamb had unfolded it. Glancing at the headlines, Lamb turned to Anna, who walked beside him. "It's quite the accomplishment," he said, turning the paper to show her the cover. "Roger Williams and Lewis Yancey broke the over-water flying record flying from Old Orchard Beach, Maine, to Santander, Spain," he read aloud. "The 3,400 mile flight took 31 hours and 30 minutes."

But Anna was not listening. She was wary of the crowds. Having grown up in Brooklyn as a woman of means, she had been approached by would-be thieves on more than one occasion. The first time, the young immigrant surrendered the money she had on her person. But she never let anyone take advantage of her again. The few occasions when she was taken by surprise, Anna was more than able to resist, yelling, screaming, and even fighting back. She had left more than one assailant with a bloody nose or black eye.

Anna knew that this mass of distracted humanity was a prime target for pickpockets, and she eyed the passersby closely. The doctor seemed heedless of the potential dangers of their surroundings, so she took it upon herself to be diligent.

"We need to take the IRT subway to get to Brooklyn," she said as she handed him his suitcase, took hold of Lamb's arm, and guided him through the crowd toward the tunnel to the Interborough Rapid Transit platforms. "It will take a couple of hours to get to the Teplow house in Bushwick. We will need to change trains at Canal Street."

"How do you know so much about the subway?" Lamb asked, looking up from his newspaper when the light dimmed as they entered the tunnel.

"I lived in Brighton Beach when I first came to America," she replied. "I took the subway to Manhattan several times before I moved to Wellersburg." The tunnel was choked with passengers from a train that had debarked on the platform before them. The commuters were as rude as she remembered, shouldering their way past the pair and complaining about their luggage. Anna gave as good as she got, and with some effort, they traversed the tunnel to an alcove containing a stairway that went over two pairs of tracks to the downtown platform. As they crossed the bridge over the tracks, Anna heard the growing rumbling of approaching trains. When they descended onto the platform, there was a crowd of people there. Anna and Lamb put their bags down.

The uptown train appeared first, rumbling through the station at a rapid pace. Anna glanced at the passengers. Most were just looking forward. Some were reading. Anna made eye contact with a child who waved at her. She smiled as she watched the last car disappear through the next tunnel.

When she looked back, the opposite platform was gone. Instead, she saw a flat, barren, rocky plain. In the distance was a line of tall mountains beneath a pink sky with an enormous full moon hovering over them. Anna was mesmerized by the scene. The landscape was completely empty, save for two massive, rough, brownish-green pillars perhaps fifty feet past the tracks.

As she took in the strange scenery, a shadow passed over her. Looking up, she realized that the two pillars were in fact scaly legs. Directing her gaze higher, she saw a giant, humanoid torso sitting atop of them. Two lanky arms stretched out to the sides ending in clawed hands. One of them turned its palm toward her revealing a large, malevolent eye in its center. The shadow passed over again and Anna followed the torso up to a hairless head bearing an enormous, red, elephantine trunk that whipped around in the air chaotically.

Suddenly, the downtown train emerged from its tunnel with a deafening toot of its horn and sped by, capturing Anna's attention. A few seconds later, it disappeared into the downtown express tunnel, and Anna was again looking at the uptown platform. A handful of people stood about waiting for the next train.

Anna looked to the doctor, but his head was buried in his newspaper. He had missed the whole scene. Unless she had imagined it. The doctor noticed her glancing at him.

"Are you alright?" he asked with an expression of friendly concern. "You look like you saw a ghost."

"Something like that," she replied and quickly glanced at the newspaper to deflect his question. "What has you so engrossed in the paper?" Lamb glanced from Anna to the paper and back.

"Oh," he said, indicating a small article on one of the interior pages. "There's an article about Brian Teplow here. It says that his agent, Woody Frank, has not been seen in over a week. Unnamed sources suggest that he may have been the victim of foul play." He pointed to the article, but Anna's attention was attracted to an advertisement at the bottom of the page. Next to the "Church of Cosmic Understanding" was a familiar image.

"Does that look familiar?" Anna asked, tapping the ad with her finger. Lamb's eyes widened.

"Arthur Cophen showed me that symbol when we first met at O'Malley's church. He didn't offer to help you until after we had said that we hadn't seen it before."

"We will have to look into that after we meet with Mrs. Teplow," Anna said. The doctor nodded his agreement as the lights from their train crept out from the tunnel to their left. They pressed into the crowd when the doors opened and boarded, but there were no seats available. They migrated to the open space in the center of the car.

Ten minutes later, the train stopped at Canal Street. This time, Lamb ushered Anna and their luggage through the crowded car and onto the platform just before the doors closed. They were being herded with the mass of travelers toward the exit when Anna diverted the pair to a stairwell leading down. Once out of the steady stream of people, the noise level dropped significantly.

"This way leads to the Brooklyn trains," Anna said to the doctor. "We need to find the train that goes to," she glanced at the sheet Feldman had given them before departing, "Halsey Street on the Broadway Line."

Descending the steps, they found themselves on a long, practically-empty platform, illuminated periodically by electric lamps in the ceiling. Painted on the wall beneath one were the words "BMT BRIGHTON BEACH LINE," and beneath that was "EASTBOUND." Another sign said "BMT BROADWAY LINE," with an arrow indicating the far side of the platform.

"Our train appears to be that way," Lamb said, pointing at the sign. Anna casually lowered his hand. The doctor was acting like every tourist who came to the city and made an attractive target for unsavory elements. The two proceeded down the platform. The alternating light and dark seemed to make the platform extend continuously.

They had progressed out of sight of both ends of the platform when an unseen man, his worn and disheveled clothing stained to match the dust-covered patina of the platform, burst up from the shadows, pointing at Anna and the doctor.

"It can't be!" he cried. "I saw you die! You and Khan-Tral and Deb-Roh." The man rubbed his face with his hands neurotically. "At the mercy of Gho-Bazh!" He shuddered. "I saw you blasted by them Pointee bolts in the Dirge!"

The man backed away in the direction the pair were heading. They continued down the platform, ignoring the man, who disappeared into a gap in the wall. As they passed, they saw him rummaging through a Great War-era backpack.

"What an odd fellow," Lamb said with curious expression. Anna was taken aback. She stopped and stared at the doctor with an expression of disgust.

"After the war, New York was flooded with returning soldiers," she said clearly and directly. "The war changed a great many men. Some of them found themselves shunned and made homes in the subway." She was about to continue when the vagrant grabbed her shoulder and pushed his way between them. In his hand he held a weathered piece of animal skin parchment with an almost-lifelike black and white drawing of five people.

"See," the man said with a hopeful expression, his demeanor now amicable. "We were all there." The figures in the drawing were dressed for an overland expedition in a mountainous terrain. "You remember me," he said, pointing at one of the figures, "don't you?" At their blank expressions, he added, "Ganon. Do you remember now?"

"I'm afraid you have us confused with someone else," Lamb said politely. Ganon put the drawing in front of his face and pointed.

"That's you, Nab," he said, directing the doctor to a largish figure standing next to the figure Ganon had indicated as himself. "We were like this," he said, crossing his fingers in the doctor's face. Anna started to turn away when the man grabbed her wrist and thrust the drawing at her. "And that's you, Nygof." He pointed to the shorter of the two women in the group. "The five of us set out across the Endless Barrens in search of Khan-Tral and Deb-Roh." He put his hands on their shoulders. "I thought I was the only survivor, but now that you're here I can see my prayers were answered!" Anna took the drawing and moved near a lamp to examine it more closely.

"You're not going to entertain this man's delusions, are you?" Lamb asked incredulously. Anna pointed to the woman. Stature-wise, it was the correct proportions for her, and the correct height in comparison with the figure identified as Lamb. The figures were barely visible, but the scars on the side of her face from the creature Cophen had banished in Wellersburg were plainly visible in the image. She turned to Ganon.

"Ganon, yes?" The man nodded. "Where can we find you? I would like to continue our conversation later."

"You can't be serious?" the doctor interjected.

"I got nowhere to be, Nygof," Ganon said with a smile. "I could come with you!"

"My name is Anna," she replied politely after glaring at Lamb, "and this is Harry. I'm afraid that we have an appointment to make, but I would like to see you later."

"I could come and wait outside…"

"No, Ganon," Anna said firmly. "We need to prepare for our meeting on our journey. Where can we find you later?" Ganon looked disappointed.

"I'll be here, I guess." He thought a moment. "But you'll be coming back, so I'll wait on the other platform," he said, pointing across the tracks.

"That would be perfect," Anna said calmly. "I do not know how long we will be, but we will come back later and find you." Ganon nodded and bowed, sitting in the darkness against the wall, where his garments camouflaged him almost perfectly.

They proceeded down the platform in silence, neither speaking to the other. Eventually they reached a stairway with a sign bearing "BMT BROADWAY LINE" with an arrow indicating to go up. Lamb led the way. Once they had ascended out of view of the platform, the doctor turned on Anna.

"Are you insane?" he said emphatically, in a hushed tone. "Why did you encourage that man."

Anna glared at him. "First," she said, holding up a finger, "a little compassion does not cost anything. Second," she held up another finger, "it was clearly me in that drawing. It had my scars." Lamb looked incredulous. "I have seen frescoes and paintings that were less exact than that drawing, Anna continued" Lamb was still not convinced. "And there is something about the names he used for us that reminded me of something, though I cannot place it right now."

"Fine," the doctor conceded. "He probably won't be there when we get back anyway. If we even come back through here again." He turned and continued up the stairs.

◆

At the top of the stairs, the platform was in between two tracks in each direction. A sign on a pillar indicated that the track to their right was eastbound, and the doors closed just as they reached the top of the steps. Lamb stepped forward to the nearest door, and set his suitcase down on the tiled floor. When he looked up, a woman inside the car started yelling and pointing at the doctor. As the train started moving she frantically continued toward the back of the car. Lamb could make out the words "behind you" as the train accelerated into the tunnel.

Lamb turned around to see a well-dressed man with a Homburg hat and briefcase standing a few paces behind him reading a newspaper. He did not seem to notice the doctor's gaze. Anna approached a moment later.

"Would you have left without me?" she asked with irritation. The man with the newspaper looked up and quickly stepped aside to allow her to pass. Lamb glanced at her suitcase and realized that she had probably struggled to get it up the stairs.

"I'm sorry," he said. "No, I wouldn't have left you here, Anna." A few minutes later, an eastbound BMT Broadway Line train arrived at the platform. "Allow me to take your suitcase." Anna resisted for a brief moment, and then agreed. They boarded the train and the doors closed.

Chapter 3

July 11, 1929

It was nearly noon when Anna and Lamb found themselves on the steps leading up to the front door of a small, three-story house in the center of a row of identical houses. The lowest level was situated such that the barred windows flanked the brick staircase on either side. They were both sweating in Brooklyn's July heat, and Anna stopped Lamb from pressing the button for the doorbell so she could remove a mirror and some foundation from her purse to touch up the covering of her scars. She did not want to scare Mrs. Teplow.

Before she finished, the two were overcome by a cloud of fragrance as an older woman opened the door. She was dressed in an elegant green evening gown and held an unlit cigarette in a long holder. A large pendant hung from a necklace of shiny green stones that matched the dress.

"Are you the man from the university?" she said to Lamb in a poorly-concealed Brooklyn accent. She acknowledged Anna's presence with a brief nod.

"Yes," Anna quickly responded. "I am Dr. Anna Rykov, and this is Dr. Harold Lamb. We are from Reister University in Wellersburg." She held out her hand. The woman was flustered, but quickly regained her composure.

"Of course," she replied. "I'm Maureen Teplow, Brian's mother." She took a breath and smiled. "Wow! A lady professor," she said in her natural Brooklyn accent. Then she nodded, collected herself, and gestured inside. "Won't you come in," she added, attempting to hide her accent again.

Anna and Lamb entered, and Mrs. Teplow directed them to a living room. Anna noticed scratches in the floor indicating where furniture had been moved recently. In the center of the room was a cherrywood coffee table on top of a tiger skin rug. Two expensive-looking leather sofas, too large for the room and incongruous with the tiger skin, flanked it on other side.

Anna took a seat on the sofa facing the fireplace. On the mantle were curios from around the world, including a jade vase and an ivory figurine of an elephant. On the wall nearest the front door stood a large, gold-framed mirror that reflected the image of a famous oil painting that Anna recognized but could not identify, hanging on the opposite wall. Lamb walked around the back of the sofa and sat next to Anna.

Mrs. Teplow returned from another room carrying a tray of finger sandwiches, as well as some crystal goblets and a matching decanter containing what looked like red wine. When she saw where her guests had sat, she grimaced, but then quickly adopted a gracious smile and set the tray on the coffee table.

"May I pour?" she asked as she picked up the decanter and removed the stopper.

"Mrs. Teplow," Anna said with a smile as she put her hand over the top of the goblet nearest her, "you do not need to impress us. We are normal people just like you." Lamb nodded with a smile. The older woman looked confused. Then she set the decanter and stopper down on the tray and slumped into the opposite sofa. All of her airs vanished, and the stressed, anxious woman beneath the facade was exposed. The doctor took a small notebook and pencil from his jacket pocket.

"I've been so worried," Teplow said, her hands rising to her cheeks. "Brian has been missing for two weeks!" She glanced from Anna to Lamb and back as tears welled up in her eyes. "The police have had no leads, and they haven't told me anything in three days." She started to bite at a fingernail.

"Tell us about Brian," Lamb said calmly. "When did his 'gift' first appear?" The old woman visibly relaxed having something else to think about.

"Brian was a normal boy," she said, looking about the room. "His father bought this house when I got pregnant. Of course, it wasn't this nice back then."

"You have quite an eclectic collection," Anna said. When Teplow looked confused, she added, "Your furnishings are quite varied in style."

"Well, yes," Teplow replied. "Brian brought me back things from all of his travels." Her face grew tense again. "The trips he's taken since the second incident."

"What kind of 'incident?'" Lamb asked politely.

"When Brian was twelve he collapsed and was unconscious in the hospital for almost nine months."

"What caused the collapse?" the doctor asked more urgently.

"We never found out," Mrs. Teplow replied. "He had started having bad dreams a few months before that. At first he just tossed and turned, then he started talking in his sleep. One night he started shouting. I came to him and it looked like he was wide awake." She put her hand to her face, looking blankly forward. "His eyes were wide open and his face was a fearful sight."

She started breathing heavily. Anna crossed to the other sofa, sat next to her, and gently took Mrs. Teplow's hand. That seemed to restore the woman's composure. All the while, Lamb wrote hastily in his notebook.

"But he was asleep," the old woman continued. "He stopped shouting after a while and closed his eyes, but when he didn't wake up the next day I called a doctor, and Brian was taken to Brooklyn Hospital."

"And he was unconscious for nine months?" Lamb asked in a professional tone. "He never woke up in all that time?" Teplow thought for a moment. She held Anna's hand tightly.

"I think he came to a couple of times," she said, "but not for a while. The first time was about a month later." She looked forward in contemplation. "Yes. It was April 22nd, 1915. I remember, it was almost midnight, and we would have had to leave the hospital if he didn't show any progress." She smiled. "He woke up just in time."

"So Brian was allowed to stay in the hospital?" Anna asked.

"Yes. He was lucky. A specialist from Manhattan had heard about his case and instructed the hospital to keep him there."

"What was his name?" Lamb asked.

"It was Faeber. Dr. Gabriel Faeber."

"And what was his interest?" the doctor continued.

"He wanted to hypnotize Brian and write down what he talked about."

"Indeed," Lamb said skeptically.

Anna glanced at him disapprovingly. "Interesting," Anna said. "Dr. Faeber is a psychiatrist?"

"Yes," Mrs. Teplow replied. "He was a colleague of Sigmund Freud," she added, visibly proud of this information.

"And this Dr. Faeber is dead?" Anna asked.

"No," Mrs. Teplow replied. "He has an office in Manhattan. Brian went to see him there after his second episode. It was during one of those sessions with Dr. Faeber that his gift appeared."

"What happened?" Anna asked with interest.

"Well, I wasn't there. Brian told me about it later." Mrs. Teplow looked to the ceiling for a moment, collecting her thoughts. "As I recall," she began, turning back to Anna, "Brian said that it was at the end of the session. Dr. Faeber had just brought him back to wakefulness. Brian asked to see the pocket watch that he used to hypnotize him.

"When Brian took hold of the watch, he said that details about the doctor's father and grandfather, who they had never discussed, came to him." She glanced at Lamb with a look of astonishment. The doctor's expression remained neutral, but Anna was intrigued.

"What kind of details?" she asked with interest.

"Brian said he knew birthdays," she strained to remember. "I think he said he knew about Faeber's dachshund, Wurst, and that it was named after his childhood pet."

"These are all things that could have come up in their conversations," Lamb said dismissively. "Or he could have researched them in advance of the session."

"Are you suggesting that my boy is a fraud?" Mrs. Teplow fumed, all pretense of culture and civility gone. "He knew details about the doctor's childhood home in Germany that Faeber had to contact relatives still there to verify!"

"And this was the start of Brian's fabulous career?" Anna said with enthusiasm to break the tension. Mrs. Teplow was disoriented for a moment before she turned back to Anna.

"Yes," she replied with a smile. "Somehow, Woody Frank heard about it and signed Brian up for a management contract." Her enthusiasm waned. "Of course, he then went on tour, first on the east coast, and then Europe." She sighed. "He was gone for three years." Then a modest smile returned. "He sent me all these nice things from each of his stops," she added, gesturing to the mismatched collection that filled the room.

"You said that Dr. Faeber intervened when Brian awakened after the first incident," Lamb asked, "and he continued to see your son after the second event. When was the last time they had an appointment?"

"I don't know," Mrs. Teplow replied evenly. "Brian has been very busy. I haven't seen him myself in almost six months." She turned to Anna. "I've had to settle for telephone calls. The last one was about a month ago."

"Tell us about Brian," Anna said with a smile.

"As I said, Brian was a normal boy." The older woman relaxed, thinking of pleasant times. "He was the shy and quiet type."

"Did he have a lot of friends?" Anna prompted.

"No, he didn't." She conceded. "Not that he was strange or anything. He just wasn't outgoing. He had a couple of friends in school, but only a few, at least that I knew about."

"What did he like to do?" Anna wanted to keep Mrs. Teplow talking. She knew from her field work that you had to prime the pump. Once people got comfortable talking, the real information would flow.

"Brian was a creative boy," she replied with an expression of motherly pride. "He used to draw pictures and write stories, but he never shared them."

"Why was that?"

"I think he was afraid of being embarrassed. He wrote them in locked journals and hid them under his mattress." Teplow grinned. "At least until there were so many that he couldn't sleep in it as it was so lumpy. Then he put them in his bookcase. They filled an entire shelf almost."

"Did you ever read them?" The old woman looked sheepish.

"I didn't want to impose on his privacy," she started, "but one time he fell asleep mid-sentence, and the book was open on the bed next to him." She thought for a moment. "He must have been nine or ten."

"What had he written?" Lamb asked, his interest suddenly piqued.

"It was some kind of fantasy about a city of devils."

Anna was intrigued. "A city of devils?"

"I don't think he called them devils, but they seemed so from his description." She squinted, thinking back to that time. "If I remember right, he said they were tall and had short, curved horns and hooved feet. And big eyes that glowed red in the light!" Then an idea came to Teplow. "You know, those books are still up in his room. Do you want to see them?"

"Yes, please," Anna replied with unconcealed enthusiasm. "I would very much like to see what Brian wrote."

Chapter 4

July 11, 1929

Maureen Teplow opened the door to the upstairs bedroom and stepped inside, followed by Anna and the doctor. The room was larger than Anna had expected. The upstairs consisted of two bedrooms on either side of a bathroom. The smaller of the two had been Brian's.

"Of course, he hasn't lived here since he became famous. He has an apartment in Manhattan." The door was in the center of the wall facing a gabled window. On one side was an old but serviceable, twin bed. On the opposite side was a desk flanked by a pair of dressers with shelves of books on top of them.

Anna examined the walls. Beneath a central molding that ran the circumference of the room, the walls were covered with a child's drawings of knights and soldiers battling Napoleonic cavalry or dragons, and other fearsome beasts. Above the molding, much better quality drawings depicted a recurring pair of figures, one large and muscular, the other small and wiry, in various scenes.

"Did Brian draw all of these?" she said, sweeping her hand around to indicate all of the drawings.

"Yes," the older woman replied with pride. "My Brian is a very talented artist." She glanced around the room. "The ones closer to the floor are from when he was little."

"Indeed," Anna said approvingly. "You can see the improvement over the years as you follow them from the floor to the ceiling."

"Brian arranged them that way himself when he was five."

Lamb looked over the bookcases. The highest shelf on each was filled with locked diaries. The ones to the left had black covers, while the ones on the right were brown. The other shelves contained a vast array of fantasy and adventure novels by the likes of Sir Arthur Conan Doyle, Jules Verne, H.G. Wells, and Edgar Rice Burroughs, as well as stacks of well-read *Adventure*, *Argosy*, *Amazing Stories*, and *National Geographic* magazines from roughly 1912 through 1920. The doctor pulled one of the brown volumes from the shelf. The outside cover was completely empty. The simple lock on the book would be easy to bypass.

"Mrs. Teplow," he said, "would it be all right with you if we looked at Brian's journals?"

"The keys were lost long ago," she replied.

"That won't be a problem," Lamb said, approaching her with the journal. "These are very simple locks. A pocket knife would be able to circumvent them without damaging the book." Mrs. Teplow glanced from the book to Lamb to Anna and back.

"We will not damage them in any way," Anna said. "Whatever we can learn about Brian's state of mind may help us find him."

"I suppose so," the older woman replied. "But those were written years ago. How would they help you find him now?"

"I think our paths have crossed before," the anthropologist replied, pointing to an almost-lifelike drawing at eye level that closely resembled her, similar to the one Ganon had shown them in the subway. "When was this one drawn?"

"Brian did that one just before his first collapse," Mrs. Teplow replied. Then her eyes widened with surprise. "That looks just like you!"

◆

Anna sat at the desk in Brian's bedroom studying one of the black journals under the desk light. Following the revelation that Brian had had a precognition of Anna, his mother granted the two access to the journals, providing that they did not take any of them with them. She went so far as to provide some notebooks and pencils, as well as milk and homemade cookies, which she replenished each time she came to check up on her guests.

Fortunately, Brian's handwriting was legible. Anna had perused the black-bound journals while Lamb went through the brown ones. The locks had been easy enough for Anna to bypass with a paper clip. The black binders were the most recent. According to his mother, the black journals were written in the year or two before Brian's first illness. The brown journals dated back to his early adolescence, approximately between ages eight and twelve.

The brown binders contained amateurish tales of conventional heroes, such as knights slaying dragons, and expeditions into jungles fighting dinosaurs and giant beasts. Many were derivative of each other. Most were unfinished. The doctor found them tedious and predictable, as expected of a juvenile imagination.

The black volumes had Anna's rapt attention. They contained a series of well-crafted stories about a duo called Khan-Tral and Deb-Roh. They were set in a wondrous realm called Siashutara. In the stories, Khan-Tral was a mighty adventurer dressed in leather and furs who carried a great sword called Nightbane, the Razor of Delusions. Deb-Roh was a small but resourceful man The stories were Deb-Roh's chronicles, much like Watson's accounts of Sherlock Holmes' cases. Together, the two wandered throughout Siashutara, righting wrongs and doing good wherever they went.

"Has Dr. Faeber seen any of these journals?" Lamb asked Mrs. Teplow when she returned on one of her trips to refresh the milk and cookies.

"No, he hasn't," she replied. "I don't think anyone has read them before. You are the first!"

"These stories are quite good," Anna said, indicating the black volumes. "Brian should think about submitting them for publication." She gestured to the stacks of magazines. "I would think that these publications might show an interest in them. Especially given his celebrity."

"Those are the ones he wrote after he came home from the hospital that first time." Her expression became guarded. "He was different then," she added blankly.

"How so?" Lamb asked. His face showed professional concern. Mrs. Teplow sighed and sat on the corner of the bed.

"Before his father died, Brian was a normal, outgoing child." She smiled as pleasant memories came to her. "They would play ball in the street. It wasn't so busy back then," she added quickly. "Charles and Brian used to go 'camping in the woods' in the summer. That's what they called it. They took their bedrolls and a picnic basket down to Highland Park and stayed there until he fell asleep in the evening.

"That all changed when Charles was hit by that carriage." The older woman anticipated Anna's question and said, "That was when Brian was nine years old. He didn't see it, thank the Lord, but his spirit was broken after that. He became quiet, and spent a lot of time alone in his room writing his stories." The themes in the brown volumes made sense to Lamb now. The figure of Brian's father performing various heroic deeds.

"Those magazines were the only thing Brian looked forward to in those days," Mrs. Teplow continued. "He started having his nightmares around that time as well. I thought he was working out the passing of his father, so I comforted him as best I could. I thought it would pass eventually."

"But it did not," Anna probed.

"No," the older woman replied. Her composure was failing. "It got worse. First it was just tossing and turning. Then he started talking in his sleep."

"What did he say?" Lamb asked.

"It was just gibberish. Things like oh golly, nib, or maybe nub, canned something, gaining, and nighty or nightly came up a lot." Anna gave Lamb a furtive and knowing glance, but the doctor did not seem to have made the connection Anna had.

Their host suddenly looked very tired. Anna set the volume she held down on the desk and walked over to Mrs. Teplow.

"You should rest, Mrs. Teplow," she said, taking the woman's hands in hers. "I promise you we will take care of the journals, and we will wake you before we leave."

"You can trust us, ma'am," Lamb added.

Mrs. Teplow glanced from Lamb to Anna. "I'll just sit for a while in the living room." She rose slowly with Anna's assistance. "Just call if you need anything." Anna went with her out the bedroom door and down the stairs. She followed her host to a large arm chair.

On the side table next to the chair was a framed photograph of three people: a young man with a pretty young woman on one side, and an older man in a bowler hat on the other. Mrs. Teplow noticed Anna looking at it. "That's Brian. The girl is

Liv Lee," she said, looking upward in an expression of disbelief, 'an actress.' The man is Brian's agent, Mr. Frank."

◆

After making Mrs. Teplow a cup of tea, Anna returned to Brian's bedroom. She found Lamb flipping through a pad of plain paper she had not seen.

"I saw this," he said, pointing to another almost-lifelike pencil drawing, "at the farm in Stuckley!" The image was of the large, amorphous, greenish-brown blob that Lamb had seen during the ritual at the farm. In the picture he saw the arms, legs, giant eyes, humanoid and animal faces, and long, slippery-looking tentacles whipping around in all directions. "That is the exact thing I saw at the farm." From his expression, Anna could see that he was serious.

"None of the journals I looked at had pictures in them," she said.

"This was in the drawer," Lamb replied, indicating the open desk drawer. It was neatly arranged with various pencils, erasers, a ruler, and other writing implements. Anna took the pad and examined the drawing. Suddenly, she pointed in the background, where the head of Arthur Cophen, huge tongue lolling out, could be seen behind the massive thing in the center.

"This is not an image like your vision," Anna said with astonishment, "this is your experience! Drawn ten years before you lived it!" She flipped through the pages from the beginning. A few pages later, she gasped. The drawing displayed the barren, flat, rocky plain she had seen in the subway, including the line of tall mountains, the pink sky, and that enormous full moon. As before, she had to view the landscape before the gigantic, monstrous, scaly humanoid with the enormous red trunk became apparent. And as before, the eyes in the palms of the enormous clawed hands seemed to be looking right at her. "And I saw this exact scene briefly in the subway right before we met Ganon!"

They were posing as if for a photograph. A photograph! That was why the images were so lifelike. Somehow photographs were turned into these drawings. Photographs taken in the realm of Brian's dreams!

"We need to find Ganon," Anna said as she closed the book and put it in her purse.

Chapter 5

July 11, 1929

It was nearly six o'clock when Anna and Lamb left the Teplow home. Anna had awakened Mrs. Teplow on the sofa and informed her that they would be making inquiries in Manhattan.

"You'll call me if you learn anything?" The worry returned to the old mother's eyes.

"Of course we will," Anna said with a smile, holding the old woman's hands in hers. "We will keep you appraised of our progress. We will call you tomorrow." Anna held up the notebook in which Mrs. Teplow had written her telephone number on the inside cover.

They politely refused Mrs. Teplow's offer to make them dinner, citing that they had filled up on the milk and cookies that had steadily flowed from Mrs. Teplow's oven. Still, she handed the doctor a tin of a still-warm batch to take with him as they left.

◆

Once they rounded the corner out of view of Mrs. Teplow, who had watched them as they walked away, Lamb turned and faced Anna.

"There's a lot more going on here than it appeared," he said anxiously. "How did Brian Teplow see events in the future? And how did he draw them so accurately? And from other people's perspectives?"

"What is more important," Anna replied, "is that we feature prominently in his visions." She continued walking and Lamb caught up with her. "I have seen several brief visions myself since we set out on this trip."

"What kind of visions?" Lamb's anxiety was growing.

"On the train from Albany, I thought I saw a passing train where all of its passengers were pressed against the windows screaming in horror. But I could have been dreaming that," she added as an afterthought. "Then, right before we met Ganon, I saw that giant thing with the tentacle face in the space between the passing of two trains. The opposite platform was gone, and that rocky tundra was there instead." Lamb looked incredulous. "The landscape had a reddish-brown tone," she added insistently. "There was no vegetation, the giant was scaly and green, and the large facial tentacle was blood red. Its shadow as it passed over me is what drew my attention to it."

"What have we gotten ourselves into?" Lamb mumbled, his head drooping. Without warning, Anna turned and slapped him in the face. His anxiety was immediately replaced by bewilderment.

"I'm sorry, Harry," Anna said sympathetically, "but you are getting distracted." Before Lamb could interject, she put a finger to his lips. "It is true that there are strange things going on," she said calmly, "but we need to focus on what is real now. We are somehow involved in this strange adventure, and we need to get some answers." Lamb seemed more focused now.

Anna continued walking and Lamb followed silently until they reached the eastbound entrance to the Halsey Street subway station. The tracks were elevated over Wyckoff Avenue, and they climbed the steps after paying the five-cent fare.

"We must first find Ganon and see what he can tell us," she continued. "Then we need to talk to Brian's girlfriend and his agent. Mrs. Teplow gave me their addresses. Both of them live in Midtown, so we should get a hotel there and then talk to Ganon in private."

"You want to bring that bum to our hotel?" Lamb was indignant.

"That man knew us," Anna said as they stepped onto the westbound platform. A handful of people waited there, but no one took notice of the pair Anna lowered her voice. "He had a copy of a picture that Brian Teplow drew ten years ago that clearly depicts both of us, the possessed detective we met for the first time a few weeks ago, and Brian's girlfriend."

"Who knows where he got that?" the doctor retorted. "Maybe Brian gave him a rough draft?"

"Ganon's drawing was on some kind of canvas or animal skin. Brian Teplow did not make that. For that matter, why are his drawings so lifelike?" She paused for a moment, and then said, "I think that Brian somehow traveled to the locations in his stories, which are accounts of actual events he experienced there." Lamb was dumbfounded. "I think his 'drawings' are photographs, and the properties of that realm transform technology into simpler representations."

"That's preposterous," Lamb said, shortly before turning his back. He took several steps, shaking his head and muttering under his breath. Anna followed him and grabbed his shoulder.

"How do you explain what happened at the farm? Or that blob-thing you saw? Or Wilson Longborough transforming into several people simultaneously? And disappearing when the ritual was completed?" She turned Lamb toward her and lowered her voice. "How do you explain these scars on my face that were made by a creature that appeared out of nowhere and left no trace after being struck with a blunt silver dagger?"

Lamb closed his eyes and took several deep breaths. "This defies scientific explanation," he said with resignation. "I have no idea how to even start."

"You are thinking in concrete, rational terms," Anna said. "You need to think beyond your normal perspective as a doctor." The doctor looked skeptical. "Fear not," she added confidently. "Metaphysical matters are more my area of expertise." The sound of a horn broke the awkward silence.

"Right now, we need to get back to Canal Street and find Ganon," she said as the train slowed to a halt. It stopped short of where they stood, so they ran to the closest doors. "He said he would wait for us on the westbound, Brighton Beach platform."

◆

The Canal Street station was bustling when their train stopped at the platform between the two sets of tracks. It was just after seven o'clock. Anna and Lamb made their way with the crowd toward the steps to the Brighton Beach platforms, which needed to be traversed to reach the Manhattan trains at the other end. To his surprise, Anna took the doctor's hand and led him like a child through the tide of people.

The majority of the crowd took the first stairway which led down to the eastbound platform, but Anna and Lamb continued on to the westbound platform, which was nearly deserted. As before, the intermittent lighting on the lower level created a pattern of light and shadow. The humidity of the July heat compounded the feeling of closeness and made their clothing stick to their moist skin. Anna released the doctor's hand.

"Was that really necessary?" he said with annoyance. "I'm not a child, Anna."

"You are not familiar with the bustle of the city," she replied absently as she scanned the dark spaces along the wall for Ganon, but the platform appeared to be deserted. "I don't see him," she said with a concerned expression.

"Maybe he got picked up by the police for vagrancy," the doctor suggested, his hopefulness at the thought barely concealed. Anna scowled and resumed her search.

"He is here somewhere."

"Well, no one else is," Lamb replied, noting that last of the crowd on the opposite platform had vanished up the stairs at the far end. The tunnel was completely empty save for the two of them. And quiet. There were no sounds. No voices in the distance. No train noises. No water dripping or rats scurrying about. It was dead quiet. This disturbed the doctor, and he quickly but quietly caught up with Anna, who had kept moving.

When they were roughly equidistant from both ends, Anna felt a rush of cool air. Glancing into the darkness, she discovered a man-sized side tunnel blocked by a grate The cool air came from there.

"There is an access tunnel here," she said, pointing it out to Lamb.

"And the grate is loose." Lamb took hold of it and caught the metal lattice as it fell toward him. "The screws are broken. If anyone touched it, the cover would have just fallen off."

"That must be where Ganon went," Anna said with certainty. "We will not fit in there with our luggage. We will have to leave it here."

"You want to go down there? Just because the cover is loose?" Lamb shook his head. "The breeze is coming from there. There's probably a just big fan to improve air circulation."

"Where else could he be?" Anna asked with frustration, trying to make out anything in the darkness of the side tunnel.

"I was under the platform," Ganon said matter-of-factly. Anna jumped in surprise, Lamb reaching around to stop her from hitting her head on the lip of the opening. "There's a lot of space under there," Ganon tapped on the concrete floor, "and nobody ever looks there."

"Very resourceful," Anna said, catching her breath.

"That's me," the vagrant replied, pulling out the scroll from his coat. "That's why you hired me, Nygof. You needed someone who could find things and get you out of tight spots." He pointed at her in the drawing. "You were the leader." He pointed at Lamb. "You were the thinker." He pointed to the figure on the other side of Lamb in the drawing. "Govil was the muscle." He moved to the other woman. "And Sif was the client. Remember?"

"Perhaps we should go talk in private," Lamb said, looking about. The platform was still deserted, and there were still no sounds.

"There's nobody here," Ganon said.

Suddenly, the coolness of the side tunnel was replaced by a chill that permeated the entire tunnel. The lights dimmed, and an uneasy, electrical sensation flowed through them.

"They're back again," Ganon said warily, looking from side to side in the dark spaces.

"Who's back?" Lamb said worriedly.

"The assassins," he replied, putting his finger before his lips to signal quiet.

"What assassins?" Anna whispered.

"Gho-Bazh's assassins," Ganon replied evenly. "Been after me since I escaped. Even sent his minions all the way here." He moved away from the platform edge and started back toward the grate. "We need to hide," he said anxiously, "but they know all the secret places by now." Lamb was annoyed. This had gone on long enough. The man was clearly delusional.

"Come with us," he said, grabbing Ganon's arm to lead him toward the far stairwell. "We'll hide you where they won't think to look."

As the doctor turned in the intended direction, a cloud of inky blackness rose through the platform and congealed into a humanoid shape covered with thick, curly hair and crowned by a pair of short, curved, serrated horns.

As it became more substantial, a bipedal form with cloven hooves became apparent. The being was slightly taller than Lamb. It was covered head to foot with coarse hair. Its feet were cloven and its head was indeed crowned with a pair of short, curved horns. Its mouth was abnormally wide and lined with two rows of sharp, inward-pointed teeth, and it had large, curved, and pointed ears.

It reached out toward Ganon with triple-joined fingers, half as much longer than human fingers, that ended in bony points. As it lunged, the light struck its octagonal, dark red eyes, and they seemed to glow. They were protected by bony brow ridges and did not appear to blink.

Lamb was frozen at the sight of the thing, but Ganon pushed him aside and thrust a flashlight in the attacker's face. The red eyes glowed brightly, and then it shrieked and swung its arms blindly in search of the light.

"Come on," Ganon shouted as he pulled Lamb to his feet and down the platform. There was a gunshot from behind them. Lamb turned to see Anna holding her smoking revolver. The being was now prone on the platform, and as they watched, it started turning to smoke. "Let's go! There'll be more soon!"

Anna glanced at the vague outline of the being she shot before it too faded away and then she ran after the others. The electric sensation increased, and she could feel her hair starting to stand up. Then, several more of the inky clouds erupted from the floor, walls, and below on the tracks.

Lamb fumbled to draw his own pistol. Ganon continued to drag him toward the steps up to the Manhattan platform on the upper level. Anna followed at a run. Just short of Ganon and the doctor, but in front of Anna, a cloud consolidated into another of the beings, and another appeared, fully-formed, from below on the tracks.

Lamb fired two shots that caused the head of the one between him and Anna to explode into a vanishing cloud. At the same time, Anna feinted away from the one that had climbed up from the tracks and used the added distance to aim and fire two rapid shots into its chest. Anna's ears rang as entrails sprayed onto the track bed, briefly sparking against the third rail before they vanished. The mass of the attacker fell forward onto the platform. It reached out with its clawed fingers to rake at Anna, but fell short and exploded into a black cloud on impact with the floor, inches from her feet.

"Come on," Ganon cried as he tugged on Lamb's arm. "We need to get out into the light. They can't see good outside."

"They don't seem so tough," Lamb said as he watched more clouds form around them.

"They can't handle bullets," the vagrant shouted. "They got them energy sticks. But just as guns don't work where they're from, their sticks don't work here 'crept as clubs."

Just as Lamb and Anna emptied their weapons and dispatched the last solidified assailants, an express train, as if on cue, zoomed though on the center tracks. The gust of wind caused by its passing dissipated the still-forming clouds and allowed the three to reach the stairwell. They climbed quickly back into the heat and humidity of the crowded upper level.

◆

"What were those things?" Lamb asked, panting from the exertion of running up the stairs.

"Those were Pointees," Ganon replied, "don't you remember?" His weathered visage bore an expression of surprise and distress. "They were sent by Gho-Bazh to get me for helping Deb-Roh to escape." He looked suspiciously at Anna and Lamb. "How come they're not after you?"

"Perhaps they did not know where to find us," Anna replied quickly.

"Well they know where you are now," Ganon replied. "We best get out of here."

"We will find a hotel and talk there," she replied, steering the other two toward the Center Street exit. They milled cautiously through the crowd. Lamb looked around every now and then, but there was no sign of the extradimensional attackers or any clouds of inexplicable inky blackness.

When they reached the exit, Anna quickly made her way down the block and held up two fingers to hail a cab. A blue, Ford sedan with "TAXI" painted on the door pulled to the curb. The driver stepped out and opened the door for Anna. She climbed in, immediately followed by Ganon. Lamb and the driver stowed the luggage in the trunk.

"Where to?" the driver asked from behind the wheel after Lamb closed the rear door.

"We need a hotel in Midtown," Anna said. "Can you recommend one?"

"There's the new Hotel Lexington on 48th Street," the driver replied. "I hear that's nice."

"Take us there, please," Anna said with a smile.

"Sure thing," he said as he pulled out into traffic.

Chapter 6

July 11, 1929

Dodging cars, delivery trucks, pedestrians, and trams, they arrived at the entrance to the Hotel Lexington just as the sun was sinking below the skyscrapers to the west. A red-coated doorman opened the door of the taxi and a bellman ran up with a luggage cart to collect their bags. Lamb gave the doorman a nickel as Ganon and Anna stepped out of the cab. When he saw Ganon, the doorman started moving to stop him.

"He's with us," the doctor said, handing the man a quarter.

"Of course, sir," the doorman replied and tipped his hat at Anna. "The front desk is inside to the right." He glanced at the vagrant again and added, "The lavatories are to the left, next to the smoking lounge."

"Thank you," Anna said with a polite smile. "I will see to some rooms. Harry, take Ganon to the washroom and help him clean up a little." Lamb nodded as they passed through the revolving door into the lobby. The vast chamber beyond was decorated in reds and golds, reminiscent of an eastern palace. Settees and divans occupied a sunken space in the center of the room, beyond which a bank of elevators lined the far wall. To the right was a long marble counter, behind which a line of fashionable young women assisted guests queued up before them. To the left, nearest to the entrance, was a space decorated in deep wood and brass railings where well-dressed men and a few much-younger women sat within a cloud of tobacco smoke. Next to the smoking lounge was a pair of alcoves concealing the entrances to the men and women's washrooms. Lamb guided Ganon toward them while Anna proceeded to the right and joined the shortest line.

Suddenly, there was a commotion as sighs and hushed whispers filled the room. From one of the elevators, a petite woman in a form-fitting, low-cut white evening dress emerged. Her red hair was styled in short tight curls, and she wore a large necklace that reflected the light of the great chandelier that hung over the recessed central area. There was a stampede from the smoking lounge as the men surrounded her and started hounding the woman with questions.

Anna took advantage of the distraction to step up to the counter, followed by the bellman. A pretty blond in a Hotel Lexington blazer smiled.

"May I help you, ma'am?"

"I would like two adjacent rooms please," Anna replied pleasantly. The woman frowned.

"How long will you be staying with us?"

"A few days. We are not certain at this time." The woman bit her lip and flipped through several stacks of cards. After a moment, she perked up.

"I'm afraid that we don't have any adjacent rooms available at the moment," she said apologetically, "but we'll have a residential suite available shortly." She indicated the woman, who now preceded a string of bellmen pulling luggage carts. "Ms. Miller is leaving us." Anna did not react to the name. "That's Marylin Miller, the dancer."

"I'm afraid I am not familiar with the theater," Anna replied flatly. The woman behind the counter adopted a professional demeanor again. "The suite will be acceptable." The woman picked up a telephone and dialed.

"Housekeeping," she said. "I need suite 1806 cleaned up as soon as Ms. Miller has vacated." There was an agitated flurry on the other end. "I need the suite cleaned up immediately. Guests are waiting!" There was more chatter from the other end. "Very well. Contact me as soon as it is ready. This is Lorraine at the front desk." Lorraine hung up the telephone and noted Anna's concern. She blushed. "Ms. Miller is a... um… spirited woman. She took many liberties with the decor."

"I understand," Anna replied with a polite smile. "How long will it be before the suite is available?" The woman glanced at the large clock mounted above the elevators. It was almost nine.

"I would guess about an hour, she said, holding up a finger. "One moment, please." She picked up the telephone and dialed. "Mr. Lyons? I have guests waiting for suite 1806." The voice on the other end spoke. "Well Ms. Miller just left, and it will be at least an hour before the suite is ready for occupancy." The voice on the other end spoke again and hung up. "Mr. Lyons, the night manager, will be here shortly to take care of you until the suite is ready." She rotated a book toward Anna. "Please sign the register."

Anna took the offered pen and wrote their names. The woman retrieved the pen and rotated the book back toward herself just as a well-groomed man in a tuxedo sauntered over in front of the counter.

"Mr. Lyons, this is Doctor...?" The woman looked at the registry and then looked to Anna.

"Dr. Anna Rykov," Anna replied, taking the manager's offered hand.

"Charmed madam," Lyons said as Lamb and Ganon stepped up beside her.

"And this is Dr. Lamb and Mr. Ganon…"

"Major Ganon," Ganon interrupted.

"Major Ganon," Anna corrected. Lyons looked over Ganon, who now wore Lamb's oversized, but clean jacket. His face and hands had been washed and his wet hair was neatly combed, but he still looked out of place.

"Um, yes," the manager replied, an expression of distaste flashing across his face for an instant before his artificially professional face returned. "As it will be some time before your suite is available, the Hotel Lexington would be honored if you would accept a complimentary dinner while you wait." He glanced at Ganon again and said, "I will arrange a private dining room for your group."

"That is very kind," Lamb said with a smile.

"Not at all, sir." Lyons snapped his fingers and the bellman stepped up. "Store their belongings in the luggage room and see that it is brought to their suite as soon as it is ready!"

"Yes, sir," the bellman said as he snapped to attention. "Miss Lindsey will attend to your arrangements. Now excuse me while I make the preparations for your meal." With that, Lyons indicated the woman behind the counter and stepped hastily away.

◆

Fifteen minutes later, the three were seated at a large table in a mahogany-paneled dining room. A crystal chandelier hung over the table, which had been set for three, though it could clearly accommodate a dozen. Anna sat at one end, with Ganon and Lamb on either side. Before them was a plate of chilled oysters, pate, caviar, and small crackers. A waiter in a white jacket periodically refilled their glasses with iced tea. Having obligingly consumed Mrs. Teplow's cookies earlier, Anna and Lamb ate sparingly, but Ganon ate with abandon.

"Now, Ganon," Lamb began, "you said that this Gho-Bazh sent those cloud beings…"

"Pointees," Ganon corrected through a mouth of pate.

"Yes… Pointees to kill you? Why?"

"We helped Deb-Roh escape. He was a big prize in Gho-Bazh's fight against Utgarda." At the mention of the name, both Anna and Lamb almost choked.

"Gho-Bazh is fighting Utgarda?" Anna asked intently.

"Of course!" Ganon said through a mouthful of oyster. "Gho-Bazh wants to banish Utgarda from this world so he can have it himself. Sure, he says he's trying to save humanity from Utgarda, but wizards are all hungry for power."

"And why is Deb-Roh so important to Gho-Bazh and Utgarda?"Anna probed.

"You sure ask a lot of base-level questions for the woman that set up an expedition to rescue him," Ganon said skeptically. "Maybe you're not who I thought you were." He continued eating with abandon.

"Let's assume that our memories of the events you are referring to have been somehow erased or hidden from us," Lamb interjected. "You seem to know a lot about this world, as well as the other one. Why is that?" Ganon looked critically at the two of them before continuing.

"Because Gho-Bazh banished me back here," Ganon replied, "'stead of coming me back by myself."

"What different does that make?" Anna asked with extreme interest.

"There are two kinds of travelers," he began, stopping to swallow and take a drink before continuing. "Those who travel by choice, and those who get taken there. Those who travel by choice know both sides. Those who get taken know only one side or the other."

"So why does Gho-Bazh sending you back make a difference?" Anna's curiosity was growing.

"Because them that can travel by themselves can make up who they want to be there…"

"Like a fantastical…" Lamb interjected.

"Or heroic," Anna added, "version of themselves."

"I suppose. Ganon nodded.

"And when they return," Anna continued, "the voluntary travelers know the difference between their traveling persona and the… other one."

"That's right," Ganon said.

"But if a voluntary traveler is sent back involuntarily, they won't know who they are here?" Lamb asked, a smile slowly forming across his face as he began to catch on.

"So Ganon is your traveling persona, but you do not know your identity in this world." Anna considered this information while nibbling on some pate. "So if he banished you," Anna said inquisitively, "why is he out to get you now?"

"I don't know," Ganon replied with a shrug. "Perhaps it was so I didn't run into you."

"But clearly we have met before," Anna said, digging in her purse. She produced Brian Teplow's sketch book and flipped the pages until she found the duplicate of Ganon's drawing. The vagrant's face lit up and he covered his mouth in astonishment.

"Where," he stammered, "where did you get that?"

"This belongs to Brian Teplow," Anna said, staring intently at Ganon. "A man with an amazing imagination and gift for drawing."

"That's not imagination or a drawing," Ganon replied. "That was a picture that we got taken before we entered the Endless Barrens of None." He took the journal from Anna and laid it flat on the table. "That's you," he pointed to Anna's image. "That's you," he pointed to Lamb. "That's me, of course," he said pointing to his own face. "And that's Govil." He pointed to Cophen. "He was a sullen one, but good in a scrap."

"And the other woman?" Lamb asked. He smiled at the image, as if remembering something pleasant.

"That's Sif," Ganon replied. "You remembers, don't you? You two sure had a thing for each other."

"She does seem familiar," Lamb mused absently, staring at the image. Anna was not moved.

"And how did we all get together?" Anna asked.

"You arranged the expedition in Brynner, on the Isle of Brynn." Ganon looked for a spark of recognition. When he didn't see one, he added, "that's the usual starting point for travelers. They go off to explore from there." He pointed to Sif. "In your case, Sif was in a big hurry to find Deb-Roh, and I thought she hired you to arrange an expedition."

"And you didn't know us before then?" Lamb was puzzled.

"You and I had had some acquaintance in the past, Nab, but neither of us could remember where. When I joined up, you and Nygof and Sif was already together. You hired me as a guide, and I found Govil for protection. We got us some shufflers an' set out just after the thaws, though I told you that was a bad idea."

Ganon closed the book and put it in his lap as Lyons appeared, followed by a string of white-coated waiters carrying covered platters.

"Complements of the Hotel Lexington," Lyons said with a flourish as the waiters set the platters down on the table. "Here we have Lobster Thermidor, Prime Rib au jus, and Chicken Florentine. Enjoy." Lyons started to leave, but then turned back and said, "your suite will be ready around ten o'clock. So as soon as you are finished here, I will take you up."

"Thank you, Mr. Lyons," Anna said with a pleasant smile.

"Not at all, madam," the manager said as he closed the door behind him. The two waiters remained to serve, so the three decided to continue the conversation later in their rooms.

Chapter 7

July 11, 1929

"As I said," Ganon continued after the bellman departed, "we acquired some shufflers and set out just after the thaws, though I told you it was a bad idea."

They were seated in the living room of their suite, which consisted of two bedrooms on either side, each with a private bathroom, and a center chamber furnished with comfortable couches, a coffee table, a writing desk, and several chairs. Anna and Lamb had sat down on a couch, and then Ganon unexpectedly sat between them. He put Brian Teplow's sketchbook on the table before them.

Ganon indicated another life-like drawing near the beginning of the book that displayed six large, reptilian beasts. Two had long, scythe-like claws extending from the front pair of their six legs. The other four had three pairs of legs that ended in five clawed toes. The former two and three of the latter four were equipped with tack, saddles, and bundles strapped to their wide backs. The remaining beast was piled high with cargo. Cophen, or Govil as he was called by Ganon, held the reins of the armed beasts, while Lamb, known as Nab, and Brian Teplow's girlfriend, known as Sif, each held the reins of two of the others.

"Govil and I rode point on the males as we were experienced cavalrymen." Ganon grimaced. "Those creatures really liked Sif, but they were wary of you for some reason, Nygof."

Anna was not surprised. She had always had a negative effect on animals. Still she was amazed at the near photographic quality of the drawings. It was evident that the figures in them were Lamb, Cophen, Ganon, herself, and Liv Lee. The clothing and proportions were consistent from one drawing to the next, and the drawings seemed to follow a progression.

Ganon flipped the page to display a long, narrow stretch of land extending to a far shore in the distance. Water rippled to either side with glimpses of something poking through the surface here and there. The perspective was from a rider on the fourth beast in the line. Ahead, Sif had turned her head back and was smiling, as if for a photograph. Beyond her, another smaller figure was seated facing in the direction they were heading. Probably Anna. Before her, the two talon-limbed beasts were several paces ahead of the rest. One was rearing up on its two hind legs, its bladed forelimbs splayed forward. Its rider was facing them. He was too distant to make out who it was. The other rider was barely visible behind the cloud of dust his mount had kicked up.

"Sif sure had a shine for you, Nab," Ganon continued, "which was odd as we were out to save her beau." He gathered his thoughts. "Anyway, we left the Isle of Brynne across the Narrows a couple a days later, and about halfway across something spooked Govil and he ran off at a charge. He didn't say anything, he just charged off. So I told you to keep going at a walk while we sorted it out as we didn't want to be on the Narrows when the tide came in and the two lakes came together."

"Why was that?" Lamb inquired, totally engrossed in the story.

"The twin lakes were home to the cephalopods," Ganon said with wide eyes, "and when the tide came in, they could reach across the Narrows, grab man and beast with their tentacles, and drag them into the water never to be seen again."

"What had startled Govil?" Anna asked, refocusing Ganon.

"Well," he said as he flipped the page, "on the other end of the Narrows was a gang of 'toll-takers.' They were just bandits out for easy pickings. But they didn't count on a veteran skirmisher. No sir. By the time I got there, Govil's shuffler had gutted two footmen, while he had another impaled on his saber up in the air almost over his head." He paused for effect. "There were two or three other ones running off down the Len Lorche road. Fortunately, we were going by way of Tiornen."

"And what was our destination?" Anna said.

"We were heading for Gho-Bazh's palace at Kreipsche, but we were trying to skirt the Endless Barrens of None, as that was Utgarda's domain. The plan was to follow the trade route, but that was not to be."

"What happened?"

"We were set upon by a tribe of the Draunskur!" Ganon's expression was panicked. "They came leaping out of the sand where's they had hidden and knocked over your mount." He looked at Anna with horror. "Now those heathens were no friend to the people of Brynn, and especially to Outsiders, as they worshiped Utgarda like all the Barrens folk did, and their reputation with women was nothing to speak of in polite company."

"Well they knocked over your mount and were worrying Sif's when Nab here planted an arrow into the head of their chief. That made them really mad, and before you know it, a hundred of them are pouring over the dunes to surround us." He took a breath and his tone relaxed.

"Now you picked a good one in that Govil. That man could fight and had no fear! He took that twin-bladed beast and sliced a path through them. We were all thinking the same thing and followed right behind him. I took up the rear to fight any pursuers. I think Nab grabbed you, Nygof, because the next time I saw you, you were riding double on his mount."

"In the end, we lost two shufflers and most of our supplies since they got the pack animal too. But that distracted them enough for us to escape to Tiornen where we could resupply. Sif still had a bunch of those Pointee eyes, so we were set for cash. Lord knows where she got them all.

"But it took a couple of days to get settled that we had not planned on, and since Utgarda probably knew where we were, we had to go overland through Folly and along the other side of the Groaning Slopes of Woe."

"Why was that a problem?" Lamb asked anxiously.

"Well, Folly wasn't easily passable country, and that put us in Gho-Bazh's territory early, and at the other end of the Groaning Slopes. And instead of temperate grasslands, we were now traversing through jungle and rough country. In any event, we were able to get more supplies and another shuffler for Nygof, but we had to split the gear between us, which slowed us down."

"You said I shot the uh… chief with an arrow?" Lamb asked. "I've never shot a bow in my life."

"That's right," Ganon replied with a wide smile. "You were an expert shot, Nab. You hit that Draunskur big hat right between the eyes, and your shaft pierced right through his skull!"

"You mentioned earlier that the Pointee weapons did not work here and guns did not work there," Anna said. "Why is that?"

"I don't know," Ganon replied with a shrug. "But I misspoke. It's not that they don't work. They're not there at all. I'm sure those Pointees had their staffs when they were sent he to get me, but they didn't have them when they arrived. That's why we got the jump on them. They were empty-handed." He scratched his head.

"You were quite adept with knives and axes, Nygof. You were throwing them with precision. You could split a melon from fifty paces!" Anna examined her image in the drawing and noted the bandolier of knives over her shoulder. Ganon put his hand on Lamb's shoulder, "But Nab here was the sharpshooter. He was shooting birds out of the air and varmints without looking. Why he was the one who kept us fed! And well fed we were when he was around!"

"It sounds like the expedition fared well," Anna said with a smile. Ganon's expression turned grim.

"That was when it turned bad," he said. "A couple of days out we were trekking through the jungle. It was very wet, and the bugs were biting savagely. We were all bitten good, but Sif got sick. She was feverish and shaking. Nab pushed for us to get out of the jungle as fast as we could, but the going was slow as Govil and I had to cut a path through the ground cover."

"What happened to her?" Lamb was concerned.

"Well, you bundled her up tight, in spite of the heat, and used up nearly all our water keeping her hydrated. But, Govil came through again. He knew Folly, and found some plant life that stored water in the trunk, so we were able to extend out supply. Still, they were very uncomfortable days. It took nearly a seven day to get into the hill country. Of course, then it just got worse."

"Why?!" Anna and Lamb both cried at once.

"That was the start of Gho-Bazh's territory. As soon as we were out of the jungle, we were in danger from the Pointees. The horned devils lived underground and popped up to ambush the unexpecting. Of course, most of them don't have energy sticks. Only the ones in service to Gho-Bazh. But the primitives were tough enough. They could leap about on their hooves twenty paces at a time and lash out with those extra-long fingers. Their claws have hooks on the bottom, and when they grabbed you, they latched on and made a mighty tear in your flesh." He lifted his filthy shirt to reveal several old parallel scars that crossed from the right of his chest to the left of his abdomen.

"Those were from my campaigning days, but it was a lesson I'll not forget." He reached out and put his hand around the back of Anna's head. "Saw one reach right around a man's head like so and slice six stripes clean to the bone. Imagine my fingers half as long again." He imitated the motion.

"Six?" Lamb asked.

"Yes. Pointees have six fingers. Well, five and a thumb of sorts."

"What happened next?" Anna asked, engrossed in the tale now too.

"Well," Ganon continued after clearing his throat.. "Well, things were quiet for a couple a days. We were well into the Groaning Slopes, what with all those gullies and ravines. It was slow going, and we were trying to be sneaky, but they knew we were there all along.

"We knew they were more effective at night, so we were moving by day and taking care to set up a strong defensive position before we bedded down. Sif was no better, so we let her sleep. Nygof watched first, then Nab, then Govil, then me. About a five day in, we were attacked. We were in a wooded ravine. Tight on all sides, and we were camped under the foliage so that we were hidden from sight. But the Pointees could see heat too, and were drawn right to us. Govil was overwhelmed and taken down before he could warn us, and we were all taken."

"We had better stop here for now," Anna said after glancing at the clock on the wall. It was nearly three o'clock in the morning. "We have a busy day tomorrow, and we need to get some rest." She rose and headed for one of the bedrooms. "Good night, gentlemen."

Lamb glanced toward the other bedroom and was momentarily concerned that he would have to share with

Ganon, but when he turned back, Ganon was asleep on the sofa where he sat.

Chapter 8

July 12, 1929

Anna slept deeply for the first time since the Stuckley incident. She awoke refreshed, but had had a strange dream in which she was flying with butterflies. The dream was from her perspective, and she had felt both free and confined at the same time. The swarm started in a lush tropical forest, striking up the slopes and beyond a great snow-capped mountain range into a purple-pink sky high above a barren and rocky landscape. Her vision had been fixed downward, and she had been in a state of complete relaxation and comfort. The plain turned into frozen tundra, and at the first sign of snow, the flight turned upward into the night sky and then everything went black and she awoke.

Emerging from the bedroom in her silk pajamas and a hotel robe, she was surprised to see two men in suits sitting on the couch with their backs to her. One was reading a newspaper, and the other was savoring whatever he was eating. Anna cleared her throat, and the two men stood suddenly. Harry Lamb put down his newspaper and smiled, nodding toward the other man.

"Good morning," Lamb said.

"Good morning," said the other man. It was Ganon. He had bathed and shaved, and gotten new clothes.

"He cleans up nicely," the doctor added. "I called down and had them send up some clothing based on the sizes of what he had been wearing."

"Very nice indeed," Anna said approvingly. Tidied up and neatly dressed, she found their new companion rather dashing and exotic.

"Nab, er, Doc, said I needed to fit in better, so we can learn more about what's going on." Ganon was sheepish in his new outfit, and hastily wiped some crumbs from his shirt when he noticed them.

"You think Ganon should come with us?" Anna asked with reservation, pouring herself a cup of coffee from the pot on the coffee table. Then, she picked up a jelly-filled pastry from the adjacent plate and delicately took a sampling bite of it. The flavor agreed with her, so she took a larger bite.

"Well, we can't just leave him here," Lamb replied. "Gho-Bash seems to have a target on him. So if we leave him alone, he's likely to get attacked again. Best to clean him up and bring him with us. I already told him what we're to do."

"Right," Ganon inserted. "So Teplow is the one who drew those pictures. And he clued in that trustee fellow who set you all up for that ceremony. Then he went missin'. Sounds fishy to me."

"I also sent a telegram to Dr. Feldman," Lamb added, "informed him of our conversation with Mrs. Teplow, and gave him our address here at the hotel in case he needs to contact us."

"Very well then," Anna said after swallowing the last of the pastry. "I will put myself together, and we will go to see Mr. Frank."

◆

At 11:00, Anna, Lamb, and Ganon stepped into the elevator of the building on 53th Street. The Frank Theatrical Talent Agency was located on the 14th floor. They stood in silence along with a dozen other people, and the elevator stopped several times before reaching their floor. The wide hallway outside the elevator had a checkered tile floor and was decorated with paintings of flowers interspersed with comfortable, cushioned benches flanked by ashtrays next to each of the many office doors. Many of them had people sitting, some smoking, waiting for their turn with the occupants. At the end of the hall was a large window overlooking an alley and the fire escape of the building next door.

Anna led the way to the last door on the left. *Frank Theatrical Talent Agency* and *Woody Frank, Prop.* were painted on the frosted glass pane. Inside, she could hear typing. Anna opened the door and entered. The small, outer office was barely big enough for the large, matronly woman typing at the desk.

"I'm sorry," the, woman said without looking up, "no auditions for now. Mr. Frank is indisposed until further notice."

"Is Mr. Frank here?" Anna asked politely, accentuating her Russian accent so as to sound exotic. The woman looked up. Noting that the three were better dressed than her usual visitors and not behaving like show business hustlers, she stopped typing. Anna continued, "We are here about Brian Teplow."

"I'm afraid Mr. Frank is not available..." the secretary started to say politely when the door behind her opened and the man from the photograph in Mrs. Teplow's house appeared, an identical unlit cigar in his mouth.

"I already told the police all I know!" he shouted. "And my story was verified! So get lost!" With that, he slammed the door. The woman stood.

"As you can see," she said, rounding the desk, "Mr. Frank is not taking appointments today." She opened the door. "Good day," she added with a pleasant, but firm, demeanor, gesturing for the three to exit. Anna and Ganon complied.

"But we've been sent by his mother to look for him," Lamb said pleadingly, stopping and turning toward her in the doorway.

"Yeah, we've heard that one before. Unless you got some bonafides, we're done here." With that, the woman all but pushed the doctor out and closed the door behind him.

"That was less than productive," Lamb said dejectedly.

"Actually it was quite informative," Anna replied.

"Yes," Ganon added. "That man is scared of something."

"And he was quite clear that he was a subject of police inquiry," Anna continued, "but apparently has been ruled out." Before she could continue, a man in a brown suit and hat approached.

"Excuse me," he said politely with a strange, perhaps Scandinavian, accent, as he removed his hat. "My name is Peter Gulden, and I'm with the Eastern Mutual Life Insurance Company." He handed Anna a business card. "I understand you are looking for Brian Teplow. Mr. Frank has a large life insurance policy on Mr. Teplow, and the company has sent me to check out this 'mysterious disappearance.'" He said the last part with evident skepticism. "He wouldn't talk to me either. Perhaps we can compare notes."

Anna noticed that both Lamb and Ganon had adopted unconsciously defensive postures, and neither was smiling. The doctor had a distinctly neutral expression, while Ganon was clearly uncomfortable. Gulden, however, did not seem to notice. He was focused on Anna.

"I'm afraid that our inquiries are confidential, Mr. Gulden," she said politely. "If you will excuse us, we have other appointments." She did not wait for a reply. She walked past the newcomer, followed by Ganon, who eyed the man suspiciously, and then Lamb, who tipped his hat to the man and then prodded Ganon on.

◆

Down in the lobby, Anna pulled the men aside into an alcove and rounded on them.

"What was that about?" she asked sternly.

"Something wasn't right about that man," Lamb replied.

"Indeed," Ganon concurred. "Something rubbed me the wrong way."

"Do you know who he is?" Anna asked Ganon. He shook his head. "Then what was it?"

"It was like have I seen him before, but I can't remember where."

"I had a similar feeling," Lamb added. "His appearance was altered, but he seemed familiar. And not in a good way."

"Then perhaps we should be careful," Anna said. "We are not the only people looking for Brian Teplow. We know of the police and this Mr. Gulden. There may be other interested parties for some reason, and Gulden might have associates." Anna patted the small of her back where her revolver rested in a waistband holster beneath her jacket. "We best be prepared." Lamb nodded, tapping the left side of his chest.

"I'd better get some protection too," Ganon added worriedly.

"Do you know how to shoot?" Lamb asked.

"Well, I was in the cavalry," Ganon replied, "so I'm a saber man. But I think I get the jist of those things."

"You'll be a bit conspicuous carrying a sword," Anna said after some consideration, "but we should be able to get a smaller blade or two for you to defend yourself."

Suddenly, Anna pulled the men deeper into the alcove, pressed them against the shadowed wall, and put her finger to her mouth. A moment later, Peter Gulden glanced quickly into the alcove, and then walked hurriedly past, focused on the door to the street.

Quietly, Ganon crept to the edge of the alcove and peered toward the exit. Then he looked in the other direction and grinned. He motioned for the others to join him.

"He's out front," Ganon whispered, "but there's a door back there that probably leads to an alley." He pointed in the direction they had just come from. "If we can get past the elevators, we can sneak out that way." He peered around the corner again, and then motioned hurriedly for the others to go.

Anna led the way. She waited for a pair of women to walk past and followed closely as if she was with them. She walked to the elevators, where she mixed in with the people waiting there. When an elevator arrived, she used the milling of the crowd to sneak around a corner to an unmarked pair of double doors.

Stepping through, she nearly bumped into a man in green coveralls who was unloading a van parked at the loading dock. The man said something under his breath as he let her pass. A moment later, Lamb ran blindly through the double doors, tripped over the loaded hand truck the man was pushing, and dumped its contents.

The man was about to shout when he was bodily pushed into the van, whereupon stacked boxes collapsed on top of him, as Ganon burst through the double doors. Ganon took Anna's arm as he ran past and Lamb followed closely behind. The outer doors of the loading bay were open, and the three checked their speed and walked hurriedly down the alley.

A moment later, the door to a building on the other side of the alley opened and a man dressed as a chef came out carrying a crate of refuse. The three availed themselves of the open portal and dodged kitchen staff to emerge into the dining room of a busy restaurant. They collected themselves and then walked casually out onto 52nd Street.

Chapter 9

July 12, 1929

The address provided for Liv Lee was only a few blocks east of the Frank Theatrical Talent Agency. The narrow six-story brownstone sat in the middle of a quiet residential neighborhood on East 49th Street. As Anna, Lamb, and Ganon approached the building, they noticed several men innocuously loitering in the vicinity. One was across the street from the designated address, and the other was standing a few doors down smoking a cigarette.

"Who do you think they are?" Anna asked, smiling and gesturing casually at the buildings to conceal her inquiry. Lamb followed her gestures and observed the men. Ganon walked purposefully across the street and accosted the loiterer there. A brief scuffle broke out, and the man ran off.

Anna looked to Lamb with an expression of resignation. The other man had noticed the altercation and was smiling as he turned back to watch the door to Liv's building.

"I'll try a more subtle approach," the doctor said. "Follow my lead." He offered his arm to Anna and she linked hers through it. They stopped here and there to admire the trees, the buildings, and people. When they reach the smoking man, Lamb said with feigned ignorance, "This here is might peculiar 'midst all these skyscrapers. Don'cha think?" He directed the question to the smoking man, but the man did not respond.

"Well that ain't neighborly," Lamb continued, taunting the man. "Where we come from, folks say 'Hello' when they meet and exchange some kind words."

"Indeed," Anna added, trying to conceal her accent, "some people can be quite rude!" She glared at the man, who begrudgingly tipped his hat.

"Excuse me, folks," the man said, "but I was engrossed in my smoke here." His sincerity was lacking. "I hope you enjoy your stroll through our fair metropolis." With that, he resumed watching the doorway.

"You seem right fixated on that there door, son," Lamb said after following the man's gaze. "What's so special 'bout it?"

"My, uh…, ex-girlfriend lives there," the man replied, trying to conceal his annoyance, "an' she dropped me for no reason. I'm getting up the nerve to go up and see her."

"If you want to win the good graces of a young lady," Anna said in her best interfering-mother voice, "you should give her some distance and let her think things through." She looked into the man's face, and before he could say anything, she said, "It's been less than a week, hasn't it? Let's see. Today's Saturday. I suggest you approach her after church tomorrow and make a civil apology. Now off you go." She gestured with her hands to shoo him away and the man involuntarily complied. "Tomorrow after church," she said as he walked away, "and wear a nice suit!"

Anna smiled at Lamb as Ganon rejoined them. The smoking man rounded the corner.

"I had better wait here," Ganon volunteered, "and make sure he doesn't come back." He scanned the block. "I'll meet you over by that tree across the street when you're done." Anna and Lamb both nodded their agreement. Ganon waited for a car to pass before crossing in front of the next and made his way to a bench, where he produced a pocket knife and started slicing an apple.

"I wonder where he got those," Lamb said with a look of puzzlement.

"Ganon said that we had hired him for his ability to acquire things," Anna replied with a knowing look. Lamb thought for a moment and then grinned with understanding. They climbed the stairs to the entrance and entered the building.

◆

The apartment Liv rented was one of two on the fourth floor of the building. There was no elevator, so Anna and the doctor climbed the steps. At the fourth floor landing, they stopped and caught their breath.

The space before them was about ten feet square. On their right was the door to apartment 4A, and on the left was the one to apartment 4B. Before them was a janitor's closet. They stepped up to the door on the right and Lamb knocked.

There was a slight commotion, followed by a teary, "Just a minute." Then more subtle motions, accompanied by soft sobbing. A moment later, the door opened to reveal a brunette. Her hand was before her face holding a handkerchief. She wore a gauzy pink robe over a short, pink nightgown whose neckline revealed her ample cleavage. "I don't know what more I can tell you," she continued over shallow sobs, "but perhaps we can discover something new *together*." The last word included a hint of sensuality.

"Perhaps we can," Anna said, accentuating her accent. "We have come on behalf of Brian's mother and would like to ask you some questions."

The woman was startled when she opened her eyes and was face to face with Anna. The anthropologist could tell that the runny mascara beneath her eyes had been hastily and artificially applied, that the redness had been achieved by flicking talc in her eyes, some of which was visible on the bridge of her nose, and the tears were being applied by the handkerchief. Clearly, the woman was seeking to influence the male reporters who must have been coming to interview her for their stories.

Anna looked over to Lamb with a sarcastic expression and noticed his unflinching stare at the woman's cleavage. The woman had noticed as well and smiled sheepishly. Then her expression changed.

"Haven't we met before?" she asked the doctor with interested curiosity. Lamb mumbled something unintelligible. Anna shook her head.

"That is what we wish to discover," Anna interjected. "Are you Liv Lee, the girlfriend of Brian Teplow?"

"Ex-girlfriend," Liv replied immediately, still looking at Lamb. She turned to Anna. "I broke it off with him a couple weeks before he disappeared."

"I am Dr. Anna Rykov, and this is Dr. Harold Lamb. May we come in?"

The apartment was long and narrow. The doorway opened on one end of the long hall, across from which was a small kitchen. Liv gestured past three other doors to the living room that opened out to the right at the end, and featured a view of the street below. Anna and the doctor sat on a couch in front of a coffee table, facing the window.

Liv, seeing that the couch was also occupied by Anna, sat in a chair to Lamb's right. She tried to cozy up to Lamb across the end table between them, but one look at Anna's stoic expression eliminated any amorous overtures. Instead, she wiped away the mascara with the wet handkerchief.

"As I said before," Anna said flatly, "we are looking into Brian Teplow's disappearance on behalf of his mother, and your name has come up several times, including in some unusual circumstances."

"What do you mean unusual?" Liv asked hotly. Anna held up her hand.

"Let us work up to that," Anna replied calmly. "You say that you broke it off with Brian shortly before he disappeared. Why was that?"

Liv stared with irritation for a moment. Then her expression changed and she sighed. She opened a box on the end table and removed a cigarette and a box of matches. After a moment she gestured to Anna and the doctor to help themselves. Neither took one, but Lamb availed himself of the matchbox and lit Liv's cigarette. She looked deeply into his eyes as she leaned over to ignite the cigarette.

"I'm sure we've met before, Harry," she suddenly said in a conversational tone. "Do you go to the theater much?"

"Um, uh, no," Lamb stammered. "I'm from upstate. This is only my second time in the City," he glanced at Anna and then her purse, "but we have some things that suggest that we all knew each other once." Anna withdrew Brian's sketchbook from her purse, flipped to the page with the group drawing, and held it up before her for Liv to see.

"Where did you get that?" Liv said with astonishment. "That looks just like me. Woody won't like that. We own all rights to use my image."

"You are a client of Woody Frank?" Anna asked.

"Yeah. That's where Brian and I met." She took a puff and looked up at the ceiling dramatically. "Brian was his rising star, and I was trying to get acting jobs. I figured if I hung around them, I would get noticed."

"You would ride his celebrity to make some of your own," Lamb said.

"Exactly." Liv smiled at him. "But that didn't work. After two years of traveling around with them, Woody still hasn't gotten me a job. And now that Woody blames me for Brian's disappearance, I doubt he's even trying."

"Woody Frank thinks you had something to do with Brian's disappearance?" Anna probed.

"I don't really know," Liv confessed. "He might just be saying that to turn the press away from him toward me."

"Do you have any idea what happened to Brian?" Lamb asked.

"Not a clue." She thought for a moment. "Last time I saw him was after a session with some old guy. I think he was from upstate too. He was doing his thing in the parlor, so I had to make myself scarce in the bedroom."

"You were there when Brian met with Jason Longborough?" Anna asked with urgency. Liv leaned back, distancing herself from Anna.

"Yeah," she said after a moment, "that was his name."

"Did you hear the conversation?" Anna pressed.

"No. The bedroom is at the end of the hall at his place." She shook her head. "Besides, all that hocus pocus mumbo jumbo wasn't my scene."

"You don't believe Brian has powers?" Lamb asked.

"A lot of people say that he does," Liv replied with skepticism, "but that Houdini guy said that all that psychic stuff is hooey. And he was no fake."

"If you didn't believe in him," Anna asked, "why did you stay with Brian for so long?"

"Like I said, Brian was the big star, and I was trying to get recognized. But for all that time together, nothing." She shrugged. "His disappearance has been the best thing to happen to me."

"You realize that that gives you a motive for foul play," Lamb said.

"Nah," Liv replied with a wave of her had, "The cops have been over that a hundred times. They got no reason to suspect me." She looked from the doctor to Anna and back. "And I had nothing to do with it!"

"Let's get back to the drawing," Anna said, redirecting Liv's attention to the sketch book, which she put on the coffee table. "This drawing clearly shows the three of us, but we have never, to our knowledge, met before." As an afterthought she added, "Oh yes. These drawings were made by Brian Teplow… ten years ago."

"That was long before I met him," Liv said in amazement. She picked up the sketchbook despite Anna's objections and examined the image closely. "I've never worn my hair like that, or clothes like that. Maybe's it's a lookalike."

"Does the name Sif mean anything to you?" Anna asked.

"Sure," Liv replied immediately. "I played Sif in that Viking thing at the Imperial back in '26. That was where I met Woody. He came backstage and asked to represent me, for what good that did."

"Everyone in this drawing was known by another name," Lamb said. "Yours is the first that appears to have some connection to this reality." Liv looked at him with curious skepticism.

"This book contains drawings that describe an expedition in another world," Anna said. "The expedition was sponsored by Sif," she pointed at Liv's image, "who hired Nygof," she pointed to her own image, "to assemble a team." Anna flipped the page and displayed the image of the shufflers. "Apparently, those creatures were fond of you and not me." Liv was dumbstruck. Her eyes were wide.

"You're making all this up," she said rapidly in disbelief. "Where are you getting your information from? How did you get this book?" She curled up, drawing her knees to her chest and wrapping her arms around them. "Who are you people?"

Anna held up her hands and took several deep breaths. She glanced at Lamb, who had been hesitant to move on account of the woman's overtures. At Anna's insistence, the doctor slowly reached out and took Liv's hands in his. Liv looked at him anxiously. He smiled back reassuringly. That seemed to relax her.

"Let me tell you the story of how Harry and I got involved in all this," Anna said.

Chapter 10

July 12, 1929

"I was so incensed," Lamb said with theatrical excitement, balling his fists, "that I shot the thing." He stood and mimed firing the shotgun. "I hit it square in the chest, and it was riddled with silver pellets, but there was no blood." He adopted an astonished expression. Liv was enthralled with the story, the back of her hand covering her gaping mouth.

"It was about this time," Anna interjected with equal enthusiasm, "that Cophen jumped on top of me with that enormous tongue. I struggled, but he was too heavy. I was wrestling his hands away from my blouse when that tongue wrapped around my hand and pulled it aside. I hit him in the head with my forehead," she mimed the motion, "and when he fell backward, the revolver in my waistband fell free. I got hold of the pistol and shot him several times through his mouth. The blood that sprayed from his head splattered onto the entity, which was behind him."

"All of a sudden," Lamb continued, "the pellet wounds started gushing blood. Then the thing screamed in the voices of all the forms it had taken and disappeared." He paused for effect. "After that, we poured the gasoline all over the cabin. I drove Wilson's car through the wall into the kitchen with Cophen inside. Then we cleared the building, I threw in a lit match, and the farmhouse burned to the ground"

"So this Longborough guy roped you into doing this ritual," Liv Lee said to the doctor. "You saved her," she nodded toward Anna, "from that thing, killed the monster, and cleaned up the scene. You're incredible!" She leapt to her feet and embraced the doctor affectionately.

For the past hour, Anna and Lamb had alternated back and forth telling the story of their struggle against Utgarda. As the tale continued, Liv and the doctor had gradually moved closer and closer to each other. With every part that the doctor added, Liv mentioned a related idea or notion.

"Indeed," Anna said flatly, inserting herself into their conversation. "And that brings us to your part in this affair." She smiled professionally. "As with Dr. Lamb and I, you did not know Brian Teplow when he made those drawings, which were allegedly based on his dreams."

"He was a creative guy," Liv replied, poorly concealing her annoyance. "I don't know how he did it."

"Perhaps he had latent powers even back then," the doctor offered. Liv gave him a skeptical grin. "I was as based in the rational and factual as you are, Liv, when this all started, but I can't explain what I have experienced firsthand, let alone these decade-old imaginings of his."

"Maybe you're trying too hard," Liv said coyly, taking his hand in hers and swirling her fingertip in his open palm. "You need to step back and clear your head."

"We have been pretty deep into it," the doctor conceded distractedly. Anna groaned quietly in disgust. "Maybe we should take a break."

"We need to find Brian," Anna said. "His disappearance may be related to all this, and we are all clearly part of whatever has been put into motion." She saw that her words were falling on deaf ears. Liv and Lamb were focused on each other. She was now running her fingertip up and down the tops of his fingers. Anna sighed and said, "Perhaps I will go and check on Ganon."

"Yes," the doctor said absently. "You should check on Ganon. We're going to figure how well we know each other."

"I will take Ganon and go to see Dr. Faeber at Bellevue Hospital," she said, retrieving the sketchbook from the table. "We will expect you back at the hotel." Lamb grunted, his gaze focused on Liv's eyes.

"I will show myself out," Anna said as she shouldered her purse. When neither of the other two responded, she walked briskly down the hall and out the door of the apartment.

◆

When she emerged from the front door of Liv's building, Anna scanned the street. Nothing seemed amiss, and there were no suspicious people loitering around watching the entrance. She glanced toward the bench Ganon had indicated, but there was only an old woman with a small dog sitting there.

Anna started to get concerned when she heard a "psst" coming from the alley to her right. Following the noise, she caught just a glimpse of Ganon before he disappeared back into the shadows again. Anna nonchalantly descended the steps to the sidewalk and stepped quickly, but casually toward in the direction of the alley. When she reached the mouth, she looked around, and then stepped into the shadows between the buildings.

"You were up there for a long time," Ganon said with concern. "Where's Harry?"

"He and Miss Lee are getting better acquainted," Anna replied, her eyes glancing upward in disbelief. "It seems that they are convinced that that have met before."

"And was she Sif?" Ganon's eyes sparkled and he grinned mischievously.

"Indeed she was," Anna replied. "It was a role she played in a show a few years ago." Ganon scratched his head. "I am going to pay a visit to Dr. Faeber, a psychiatrist who took an interest in Brian Teplow after his first episode of unconsciousness. Come with me. We will meet up with Harry at the hotel later." Ganon grinned. Anna sighed with begrudging acceptance.

They walked to Second Avenue and took a taxi to Bellevue Hospital.

◆

"Dr. Faeber is not available," the squat receptionist behind the desk replied to Anna's query. "He is doing his rounds and will not be back in the office until tomorrow morning."

"May I leave a message for Dr. Faeber with you?" Anna asked politely. She tore a sheet from her notebook and wrote "Need to discuss Brian Teplow case. Urgent. Please contact me at the Hotel Lexington. Dr. Anna Rykov." She folded the paper and handed the note to the receptionist. The woman unfolded the paper and read the contents.

"Why do you want to know about the Brian Teplow case?" she asked officiously.

"My colleagues and I are searching for him at the request of his mother," Anna replied, "and I am exploring avenues that the authorities may have overlooked."

"Well, I'll tell you what he told the police," the receptionist replied curtly. "Dr. Faeber does not share confidential patient information. He takes doctor-patient confidentiality very seriously."

"I respect Dr. Faeber's ethics…" Anna began, but the stout receptionist stood and pointed to the door.

"Good evening," she said firmly. Ganon was about to say something, when Anna held up her hand.

"Please deliver the note to Dr. Faeber," she replied politely. Then she turned, ushered her companion to the door, and said, "good evening," before closing it behind her.

Once in the hallway heading toward the elevator, Ganon said, "that wasn't helpful. You should have let me belt her."

"Assaulting Dr. Faeber's secretary would not ingratiate him to us," Anna replied. "Assuming that officious woman delivers our message, perhaps Dr. Faeber will contact us in the morning."

"Well, what'll we do now?" Ganon asked as they entered the elevator. There were three other passengers.

"I suggest that we go back to the hotel," Anna replied, "and you can tell me more of our experiences together." The door opened, and the elevator emptied, leaving them alone when the door closed.

"Besides," she continued, "it would be best to keep you hidden, in spite of your wonderfully-altered appearance." Ganon was puzzled for a moment, and then smiled at the complement.

◆

Anna and Ganon took a taxi up First Avenue toward the Hotel Lexington, but traffic was deadlocked by an accident near 45th Street, so they abandoned the cab and walked down 43rd Street toward Second Avenue. The sun was setting behind the tall buildings, but the evening was still warm and humid.

"Tell me more of our previous adventures," Anna asked.

"Well," Ganon began, "as I said, you assembled us all up for Sif so we could rescue Deb-Roh from Gho-Bazh. We set out as I told you, and Sif got sick just as we were entering Gho-Bazh's territory. That slowed us up and we were taken by the Pointees."

"Was that the first time we met?" Anna interjected. "How was it that I selected you?"

"You were in that bazaar in Brynner, acting like you were lost," Ganon said, "and some cutpurses tried to take your bag. Nab had gotten lost looking for something in the stalls, and you were outnumbered with just that little knife of yours." He indicated a blade about three inches long.

"Well, we were there in that bazaar too. Govil and I saw them ganging up on you, so we came to your aid."

"And I gather we were successful in thwarting the thieves?"

"Yes," Ganon replied. "As soon as they saw you weren't alone, they took off. We started talking, and you said that you were looking for someone named Sif. We'd heard of her, and knew where we last saw her, so we took you there. Along the way, it became clear to us that you were an outsider and didn't know your way around. That's when Govil pledged to protect you for some reason which wasn't like him."

"Why was that?"

"Govil was quiet and kept to himself. He didn't go out on a limb for anyone."

"And what happened to Harry, uh, Nab?"

"That was the strange thing," Ganon said with bewilderment. "We took you to the coffee bar where Sif was, and Nab was there sitting with her making like he was waiting for us!" He smiled. "Of course, he and I already knew each other…" an idea bloomed in his mind "...from the war. Yeah! That's right. We were in the war together!" He nodded his head enthusiastically. "But he wasn't in a uniform like me. He was in strange clothing… like you're wearing now!

"In any event," he continued, "they were waiting for us, and when we arrived, Sif led us to a private room upstairs all laid out for the five of us. There she told us that she wanted to rescue her beau from Gho-Bazh, that wizard from Kreipsche up in the Dirge."

"So I did not recruit you for the expedition, per se. You and Govil happened to be accompanying me when I met with Sif." Ganon nodded. "And she had been waiting for all of us."

"Yes, ma'am. She was quite worried about Deb-Roh going off with Khan-Tral to see Gho-Bazh. Like a wizard was going entertain uninvited guests or help anyone but himself."

"Why did he go?"

"Well, according to Sif, Khan-Tral said that Gho-Bazh might have had something to cure him of the nightmare visions he had been having."

"What kind of visions?"

"She said he was a seeing scenes from the past and the future. Pictures of people he didn't know and what was going to happen to them."

"And Deb-Roh did not want to see these visions anymore?"

"No ma'am. Sif said they were driving him crazy, day and night. He didn't like what he saw and they were horrible that he wouldn't share discuss them with anyone."

"And yet this Khan-Tral seemed to know about them." Anna considered the thought. "Were Deb-Roh and Khan-Tral acquainted before this journey?"

"Oh yeah! They had been long time traveling companions. They were known for annoying wizards, warlords, and monsters alike. But they had gone their parted ways for a while before Khan-Tral showed up again. When Deb-Roh and Sif got together."

"Why was that?"

"Sif said they had rescued her from the Pointees, and Khan-Tral was jealous that she fell for Deb-Roh when he had done all the work, or so he said." Ganon noted Anna's confusion. "Stories were that Khan-Tral was a great swordsman and archer, while Deb-Roh was smart and sneaky. According to Sif, Khan-Tral had distracted the Pointees while Deb-Roh freed her from her chains, but he still had to fight off the guards and was wounded in the fight. When they got back to the city, Khan-Tral stormed off."

"And Sif cared for Deb-Roh while he recovered from his injuries." Anna gave an unamused sigh. "How romantic. And when Khan-Tral returned and suggested going to Gho-Bazh, Deb-Roh was excited to renew their relationship." Ganon nodded. "When did his visions start?"

"Sif said he was hit with a spell crossing the Endless Barrens on the way back to Brynner."

"The Endless Barrens," Anna repeated. "Did you not say that the Endless Barrens were the realm of Utgarda?"

"Yes. And Gho-Bazh and Utgarda are fierce enemies."

Approaching Lexington Avenue, Anna's attention was redirected when the pair were accosted by Peter Gulden.

"Good evening, Dr. Rygov," the insurance investigator said, tipping his hat. Anna noticed that when he acknowledged Ganon, they appeared to recognize each other, but neither said anything. "Are you staying near here?"

"Good evening, Mr. Gulden," Anna replied civilly. "I was just taking an evening stroll with an old friend I have not seen in some time." She indicated Ganon and smiled. They nodded, stepped past him, and started walking again. Gulden followed.

"Have you made any headway in your inquiries about Brian Teplow?" he asked, ignoring Anna's implied dismissal. She and Ganon stopped again and faced him.

"My friend and I would like to enjoy our reunion, Mr. Gulden," Anna said politely, but firmly. "Please let us be."

"I apologize, Dr. Rygov," Gulden replied, "but Mr. Teplow has been missing for two weeks. Time is of the essence. We really need to pool our resources if we hope to find him alive." Anna glanced to Ganon, who gave her a furtive look.

"Sounds like you two have some business together," Ganon said, glancing from Anna to Gulden and back. "We can get together tomorrow, Anna. I'll come to your hotel in the morning." He glanced at Gulden as he passed and started walking in the direction they had been heading.

"I suppose you have a point, Mr. Gulden," Anna conceded.

"Perhaps we can compare notes over dinner," Gulden replied, offering her his arm. "I know a nice place not too far from here."

"Very well," Anna replied, accepting his arm. They continued to Lexington Avenue and then crossed and continued farther down 43rd Street.

Chapter 11

July 12, 1929

"I thought she would never leave," Liv said after the door closed behind Anna. She sat next to Lamb on the couch, her legs dangling over his playfully. "I feel like I have known you forever, Harry."

"I have a similar feeling toward you, Liv," Lamb replied. "But how could that be if we have never met before?"

"Tell me about yourself," the actress said, resting her chin in her palm and staring at his face. "You already said that you are from upstate."

"I am a medical resident at Reister University Hospital in Wellersburg," Lamb said. "My father was a doctor in the Albany area…"

"But you are the first Lamb to receive the modern scientific training," Liv interrupted. "Your father apprenticed with another physician, while you went to college and medical school."

"You could have guessed that." He looked at Liv's face, and noticed the bright green tint to her eyes. "You are of Persian descent." He peered intently at her. "Your father was a diplomat… for the Ottoman Empire… in Mexico."

"You could have deduced that from your medical training," she retorted with a smirk, "noting things like skin color or some telltale marks that give away tropical living in the past." She took his hand and examined the lines on his palm. "Your mother was very lenient with you." She turned his hand and looked closely. "You were an only child, and she doted on you." She grimaced. "And you were overweight as a child."

"Deduced from my relatively smooth skin," Lamb said, shaking his head, "lack of calluses or scars, and my large frame." He examined her from head to toe, stopping to admire her feminine traits, until his gaze stopped at her waist. "When the war started, you emigrated to New York…"

"Not exactly," Liv corrected. "I was sent to live with my aunt in Philadelphia, but she died from influenza in 1916, and I was out on the street. My turn." She focused on his face. "You were in the war," she said admiringly. "But you were not a doctor then. That's when you lost the weight…" she examined his physique, "and found that you liked being fit." Lamb nodded. "When you returned, you decided to study medicine."

"I had seen the horrors of the front and the primitive methods used by the field medics," he said solemnly. "I vowed, holding the remains of my closest friend, to make the world a better place by helping people."

Liv put her hand to his cheek. "You are a special man, Harry," she said softly, "but you were no model student." She gave his face a gentle slap. "You were quite a cad, and many an unsuspecting maid fell to your charms." She admired him approvingly. "And I can see why."

"Not many," he replied with modesty, "but more than a few." The doctor stared into space pretending to reminisce, and then feigned noticing Liv again. She pretended to be offended.

"You started acting in Philadelphia," Lamb continued. "You turned your panhandling into performance art, and a producer discovered you." Liv looked squarely at his face, waiting for more. Lamb concentrated, closing his eyes, and then said, "His name was Martin Beck. And that is when you met Houdini."

"How could you know that?" she said with a puzzled expression. "He had just come back to the theater after his movie experiments failed, and Marty thought I would make a good assistant for him."

"But it didn't work out," Lamb said. "You were cordial to each other, but you were too captivated by the act to distract the audience like you were supposed to."

"I never got past the rehearsals before Harry replaced me." She smiled at the memories. "But he was a swell guy, and very generous. He brought me to New York to sell souvenirs." Liv adopted a mischievous smile, opened a drawer in an armoire, and produced a pair of handcuffs. Lamb became visibly nervous. "Too much?" Liv asked with a smirk. She rose and said, "I'll be right back."

Lamb stood and looked into the drawer, which Liv had left open. Next to the handcuffs were a blindfold, some throwing knives, and a deck of cards. He turned at the sound of her footsteps and was hit by a wad of silk.

"Put that on," she said seductively and then disappeared down the hall again. He examined the bundle to discover a pair of Arabian style silk pants and matching vest. He smiled and started undressing.

When she returned to the living room, she was wearing a theatrical harem girl costume consisting of a low-cut camisole, sheer pantaloons, a sequin waistband with gold coin accents, and a hat with an attached veil. Lamb tried to resume the conversation, but her sharply-outlined eyes piercing the gauzy veil, and her inviting smile beckoned him to follow her.

◆

"So, Mr. Gulden," Anna said after they were seated, "where are you from?"

Gulden had escorted Anna to a storefront steakhouse. He had selected an open table on the wide sidewalk near the curb, but it was too hot for Anna, so she stepped through the threshold into the dining room. A plump waiter intercepted her and motioned toward a booth near the window, but the sun's rays through the glass seemed to amplify the discomfort.

At the rear of the dining room was a raised section surrounded by a rail, where a group of a dozen men in suits was being loud and boisterous. They seemed to defer to a short, red-haired man at the head of the table. The only available table was a two-seater immediately below the platform on the opposite side of the rail near the door to the kitchen. Anna seated herself with her back to the window. Gulden waited for her to sit before taking the other chair.

"I am from Sweden originally," he replied. "I came to New York from Gothenburg after the war." He signaled to the waiter using his thumb and little finger to imitate holding a mug. Before he arrived, Anna shook her head.

"Please, Mr. Gulden," she said politely, but firmly. "We are here on business. I would like to get back to my friend before it gets too late."

"Of course, Dr. Rygov," he replied. The waiter approached carrying a pair of glasses with frothy heads. "What would you would like instead, Anna?"

"Do you have lemonade?"

"Of course, madam," the waiter replied, setting one of the mugs in front of Gulden.

"You can leave both, my good man," Gulden replied before the waiter turned. He placed the second mug next to the other. "Would not want it to go to waste," he said, taking a drink. "Now, Dr. Rygov," he said after wiping the foam from his lip, "when did you meet your friend?" Anna was suspicious. "You said you had last seen each other some time ago."

"Let's talk about Mr. Teplow," she replied without emotion. "How long have you been on the case?"

"Does G'nor know Mr. Teblow?"

Anna tensed. As the waiter placed her glass of lemonade on the table, blocking Gulden's view of her, Anna reached behind her and drew the revolver from her waistband.

"Tell me who you really are, 'Mr. Gulden'," she said coldly. Gulden appeared to be surprised, but Anna could tell he was faking. "I do not recall giving you my name."

"Oh," he stammered, "I got your name from Mr. Frank' secretary."

"I thought you said that she would not speak with you."

"I went back after you left to see if she had said anything to you that she had not said to me." Anna rested her hand holding the revolver on the table.

"No, you did not. You followed us out to the elevator and lost us in the lobby. You passed by where we had hidden, and we watched you leave the building and walk down the street." Gulden started to rise. His slow movement captured the attention of some of the men behind Anna.

"I think we have a misunderstanding, Anna," Gulden said anxiously holding up his hands so that his thumbs nearly touched his shoulders. She noticed that the fingers on his left hand were twitching rhythmically. "Perhaps we should both relax and resume our meal."

Suddenly, one of the men behind Gulden shouted, "GUN!" In the next instant, Gulden dove to the floor, several of the men on the platform drew pistols, and Ganon burst through the kitchen door holding a flat stone in his hand before him. He took Anna's arm with his other hand. Two men with handkerchiefs concealing their faces pulled Thompson submachine guns out from under their long coats and opened fire toward the rear of the restaurant.

Diners scrambled away from the shooter as the rapid shots splintered the rail, the table on the platform, and struck several of the group. The men fired back with their pistols, but they were mowed down by the automatic fire.

Ganon made eye contact with Gulden, who glared malevolently and started mouthing something. Ganon thrust his arm forward with the stone out toward Gulden. The prone man's eyes glowed catlike before he turned uncomfortably away.

As Ganon pulled Anna through the kitchen door, she heard the impact of bullets following their movement and getting closer, but felt nothing when she estimated that they should have been hit. The two cleared the kitchen doorway and dove behind the brick wall separating it from the dining room. A moment later, the firing stopped, replaced by screaming, sobbing, and cries of agony. Anna turned to take a look, but Ganon pulled her toward the back door and the alley beyond.

"That was Khan-Tral! Those bullets were for you!" He kicked open the door, pushed her through, and followed. Before the door closed behind him, Ganon was punched in the face by an unseen assailant outside. The force carried his head into the wall on the other side and he slumped to the ground.

Anna was held in a tight grip from behind. The man's arms pinned hers to her side and lifted her off the ground. Another man had gotten hold of her revolver and pointed it at her face.

"Hold it," a strong voice commanded as the door opened again. Two of the diners carried the red-haired man by the arms. His torso was shredded and bloody. "Da boss is gonna wanna know who's responsible for dis!"

With that, Anna was carried and roughly thrown into the back of a car she had not noticed. The man with her pistol entered through the rear, driver's-side door and pointed the gun at her. The man who had carried her sat on her other side and closed the door behind him.

Chapter 12

July 12, 1929

"I trust your journey with us has been pleasant, Father O'Malley."

"Yes, Captain Vincenzo," O'Malley replied, "it has been a most pleasant voyage." They sat at the captain's table in the dining room of the SS Conte Grande.

"Beautiful weather and smooth sailing," Mr. Breckenridge said. "My compliments to you and your fine crew."

"Indeed, Captain," Signore Capello said in Italian-accented English, "Your people have done their utmost to make this a most relaxing and enjoyable voyage."

O'Malley had not found the journey relaxing or enjoyable. Following his report to Bishop Battaglia in Boston, the priest was surprised to receive a summons to Rome, along with a first class ticket on the SS Conte Grande to depart the following morning. He was instructed to bring any artifacts and documentation related to the "Longborough Affair" with him. He had barely had time to collect his notebooks and pack before catching the evening train to New York.

The subsequent series of interviews in the lower levels of Vatican City were most unpleasant, exhausting, and thorough, conducted in Latin to maintain even more secrecy that the isolated basement chamber provided.

"Your report is both complete and informative, Father O'Malley," Cardinal Baldassare said, closing the folder.

"Thank you, Your Eminence," the priest responded, and gave a respectful bow.

"But your activities with respect to this Longborough business have been most suspect with respect to your vows," Baldassare added with disdain. Since assuming authority over the Order of Saint Dionysius the Aeropagite, patron saint of protection from the devil, the porcine Baldassare had been on a crusade to eliminate such rites as demon hunting, exorcism, and the like from the modern church.

"These pursuits demean and belittle his Holiness's efforts to convert the pagan populations of Africa and Asia to the word of Christ by reinforcing their superstitious ways. How are we to bring these lost souls into the fold when your Order continues to promote such fantasies within our own house?"

"As Father O'Malley's report clearly documents," Archbishop Szamosközy, head of the Order, said emphatically, "supernatural activities have and continue to manifest in the mortal world." Szamosközy, a tall, hawkish man with a pointed nose, originally from Alba in Transylvania, was discounted by Baldassare and the other western Catholic leadership.

"His Holiness seeks to protect the holy word of our Savior and his apostles from dilution by those who would secularize it or diminish its divine providence." Baldassare scowled when and said, "the activities of your Order are the worst kind of propaganda disguised as doing the Lord's work."

"But his Holiness, Pope Pius XI himself, has endorsed the work of the Order of Saint Dionysius the Aeropagite," Szamosközy retorted. "And he takes a strong view of those who would reinterpret the Holy Word."

"For now, Szamosközy," Baldassare said dismissively as he stood. "In the meantime, you will keep me informed of any developments." Szamosközy and O'Malley bowed as the Cardinal left the chamber. As soon as the door closed, both relaxed.

"Don't worry about him," Szamosközy said with his aristocratic English accent. "The Cardinal is all bluster, and you are doing important work."

He moved to the side of the stone table that Baldassare had occupied and produced a small, ancient-looking chest from a hidden space there. The box was made of weathered wood and was about one foot square and perhaps six inches tall.

"I put this here before we resumed today," he said, patting the worn, but ornately painted, lid gently. It depicted a knight in a white Templar tabard holding an oblong object in both hands before him. A bolt of energy was shooting from the object, but the rest of the panel was worn away. "This box dates back to the First Crusade, but its contents are much older."

"The snake of … deceit … will restore the prophet," O'Malley said, running his finger over the inscription around the image while translating the Aramaic. "The beautiful defender will be cast aside. The dragon god... waits upon… war. The radiant warrior will fall." He looked to his superior. "This appears to be in the Kartvelian dialect of southwestern Asia."

"It was found in the mountains of eastern Nicea, now central Turkey, during the Fifth Crusade," Szamosközy replied. "Our scholars have reviewed your report and your research, and compared them to the archives maintained by the Order. They believe that elements of your investigation align with elements of this prophecy." He pulled a short sheaf of pages from his robe, along with a pair of reading glasses.

"This Utgarda," he began reading from the pages, "seems to appear across the history of human civilization. There is a trickster god, or some deific entity, seeking to lure mankind astray all over the world." He looked up at O'Malley. "As Dr. Rykov noted, Utgarda-Loki has Norse origins. Hermes or Mercury is the Greco-Roman version. Several Native American tribes ascribe the role to Coyote."

"I am aware of this, Your Excellency," O'Malley said politely.

"What you may not be aware of," the archbishop said, raising his voice to stifle the interruption, "is the existence of certain extinct pantheons and cultures that have been expunged from public knowledge." He peered at O'Malley over his spectacles like an irritated schoolmaster. "There is a deific entity that spans numerous pagan pantheons around the world. This entity has a malign intent that is never truly revealed, but those who do its bidding are said to reap unholy rewards."

"What does this have to do with Mr. Longfellow and the events in New York?" O'Malley did not understand where the lecture was going.

"This entity also takes the role of trickster god," Szamosközy continued, "and its motives are never understood. However, this entity is known to aid humanity against other entities of a non-terrestrial nature, which somehow also helps with its own agenda."

"What do you mean when you say 'non-terrestrial,' your Excellency?"

"This entity, let's use the Black Pharaoh for convenience, is said to have provided weapons and knowledge needed to defeat demons or other deities, the writings are unclear, from beyond man's realm of understanding."

O'Malley's eyes widened. "And the archivists believe that Utgarda may be an avatar of this entity."

"Yes, Sean," Szamosközy said with a nod. "They believe Utgarda may be this entity, but its motives are unclear. It may be out to help or hinder us."

"The entity said that it had to test us," O'Malley recalled. "It said it had to see if we would go through with the ritual." He thought for a moment. "It was quite unlikely that we would have dispelled it had we not happened to have extra quantities of all three ingredients. I had kept some of the powder. Lamb had made dozens of those silver pellet shells. It had sabotaged the grounding agent, so we would have failed to banish it were it not for Anna's lucky shot spraying Cophen's blood on the entity."

"Perhaps it was divine providence," Szamosközy interjected.

"Perhaps so," O'Malley continued. "Nevertheless, if we had proceeded as one might expect a normal person to, we probably would have exhausted the powder on its illusions. And I doubt we would have thought of the blood."

"So maybe Mr. Cophen was not entirely under Utgarda's control," the archbishop suggested. "Perhaps he attacked Rykov to provide that contingency?"

This gave O'Malley pause. Had Cophen been their protector, rather than an infiltrator? "What does this have to do with the box, Your Excellency?"

"This inscription speaks of five beings: the snake of deceit, the prophet, the beautiful defender, the dragon god, and the radiant warrior." He glanced at the pages again. "Our people believe, based on various references and inferences, educated guesses really, that the snake of deceit was this Brett Hanke fellow, who released Utgarda back in 1872." He consulted the notes again. "They think that your Dr. Rykov may be the beautiful defender. The dragon god may be Utgarda. And that the radiant warrior is the ultimate foe."

O'Malley examined the image on the box again. Szamosközy watched intently. When the priest looked up again, his face expressed understanding.

"The scholars believe that whatever is in this box," O'Malley said confidently, "is meant to defeat this radiant warrior." Szamosközy nodded. "What is it?"

"That is the curious part," the archbishop said. "You can see two obvious clasps, one on each of the long sides." He indicated them to O'Malley. "Note that there is a small hole immediately below each." He pointed them out. "If one were to attempt to open the latches, which are false, by the way, small needles will inject the individual with a toxin." He crossed himself and O'Malley followed suit. "We discovered this the hard way. There appears to be an inexhaustible supply."

"Now watch carefully." Szamosközy pointed out three faint depressions in the box. One on each of the long sides at one end, and one on the short side at that end. With one hand, he pressed on the two while pushing on the third. The top section of the box slid off.

Inside the box was a curious device resembling a gourd made of some kind of black metal. The surface was smooth, except for bumps about one inch in diameter and perhaps an eighth of an inch high all over its surface. O'Malley noticed some scratches in the surface.

"The composition of the device is a mystery," the archbishop said, noticing O'Malley's focus on the scratches. "The metal is unknown to earthly science."

"What does it do?"

"No one knows," Szamosközy replied. "We hope you will find out for us."

◆

O'Malley was cast from his conjectures by a loud whistle from Breckenridge and the applause of the people seated at the dining table.

"Thank you all," Vincenzo said with a gracious smile. "We should dock in New York tomorrow morning around 7:00 or so, and you should be able to disembark by 9:00. If you need to announce your arrival or make any arrangements, Mr. Moretti will be happy to send any wireless messages for you."

Chapter 13

July 12, 1929

The car stopped in an alley beside a nondescript steel door. A man in dingy coveralls holding a shotgun stood in the shadows nearby. The driver had used a variety of alleys and side streets to mask their route, and Anna had lost her bearings a while ago. Her two companions said nothing for the entire trip. The big one, who held her purse, was pressed uncomfortably close on one side, while the other never relaxed his grip on her revolver, which poked at her ribs.

As the car came to a stop, the man by the door emerged from the shadows, scanned the alley in both directions, and then stepped up and opened the car door. The big man took hold of Anna's arm and pulled her out of the car with him. Anna did not resist. The man pointing her revolver at her opened the steel door. He dragged her through the doorway into a dimly lit hallway.

They walked past the first door, which was unmarked. There were four other doors, all covered with red, leather padding. There were electric lights next to each, but only two of them were lit with the dim bulbs that provided the only illumination. Anna was taken to the first of the illuminated doorways. The big man pressed a button next to it and she heard a buzzer within. The door opened, and Anna's guide pushed her inside.

"I get extra for two, Louie," a dark-haired woman clad in a leather catsuit said as she caught Anna and directed her momentum toward a heavy steel armchair. A spoked wheel like that on a ship was mounted behind the back.

"Yeah, yeah. Tell it to the boss," Louie said in an unamused voice. Then, as an afterthought, he said, "don't do nuthin' until the boss says so." With that, he closed the door behind him, taking Anna's purse with him.

"Listen," Anna said, starting to rise from the chair. She froze at the crack of the riding crop as it struck the arm of the chair a fraction of an inch from her right hand.

"You will sit and be quiet," the leather clad woman said. Anna started to rise again. The woman grabbed her forehead from behind and pulled her back against the seat. The back of her neck struck something metallic, and a collar clamped around it.

"You can't imprison me here," Anna shouted. "I demand that you release me immediately!" Anna felt around the metal band at her neck for some kind of release mechanism, but as far as she could tell, the device was smooth and featureless.

"Now be quiet," the woman hissed, speaking slowly as if to a child.

"Where am I?" Anna started to ask, but the riding crop struck the wheel behind the chair and it clicked. Anna's voice choked off. The device had constricted slightly. She gasped for air, more from shock than a lack of breath, pulling at the metal band with her hands to no avail.

"That was your last warning," the woman said. Then, she smiled malignly and said, "If you're a good girl, I might give you a drink of water."

Fury burned in Anna's eyes, but she said nothing. Instead, she examined the room. It was exotically decorated. Racks of unpleasant-looking devices and padded manacles were hanging on the walls.

Satisfied that Anna would comply, the dominatrix walked over to a large, heavy, wooden wardrobe in the corner facing Anna. She quickly slid a small door at head height open and Anna saw a man's face. It was painted with makeup, and large spots of rouge adorned both cheeks. The eyes were heavily lined with eye shadow, and mascara enhanced his thick, dark eyelashes. His bright red lips surrounded a ball that kept his mouth open wide and whose straps disappeared around the sides of his head. The man groaned and blinked at the light. His eyes went wide in horror when he saw Anna. The dominatrix looked from him to Anna and back.

"You're lucky," she said. "If he wasn't already here, you might be in there."

Without warning, she slammed the door shut and returned to stand before Anna, who still pulled at the collar in vain. "Put your arms on the armrests," she said firmly. When Anna did not immediately comply, she stabbed Anna in the abdomen with the riding crop.

Anna cried out and her hands went immediately to her stomach. The dominatrix grabbed Anna's right arm and pushed it roughly down on the arm rest. Another metal band slapped closed around her wrist. Anna tried to resist with her left arm to no avail, and it was quickly immobilized as well. Anna was momentarily focused on her wrists, as expected, and the woman used that time to clamp her ankles to the legs of the chair.

She then smiled malignly, opened the door, turned off the light, and stepped out. The door slammed with an unnerving echo as Anna was cast into darkness.

◆

"It's strange how well we know each other," Lamb said, stroking Liv's hair as she lay with her head on his chest on the pile of cushions on the floor that served as her bed. The room was filled by a peaked canvas tent covering the walls and ceiling, and oil lamps hung strategically from the supports providing dim light.

"Indeed," she purred, caressing his naked chest with her fingers. Her lithe, naked body shuddered as he ran his finger down the indentation of her backbone. "You seem to know all about me." She slid her fingers down his side until she came to long scar just shy of his kidney. "When did you get that?" she asked lethargically.

"July 20, 1918, outside Soissons," Lamb said flatly, remembering the event. "We were on patrol in a forest when we were surprised by a German patrol. They fired a volley, and then came at us with bayonets. My closest friend, Preston Carver, was shot in the chest. He was knocked backward by the impact into my arms. The gear in his pack probably stopped the bullet from continuing into me." He stopped for a moment to regain his composure.

"Well," he continued, "I had dropped my rifle to catch him, and when the Germans charged, Preston, blood gushing from his wound, twisted to catch a thrust meant for me, and instead of skewering me, it only sliced my side."

"How did you get out of that?" Liv said excitedly.

"It was bloody," the doctor said, closing his eyes and shuddering. "I remember gunshots, and grabbing the rifle of the man who attacked me. I think I wrested it from his grip and hit him with the stock." He nodded. "Yes, I hit him squarely in the chin. I must have broken his neck." His voice faded.

"That was the first time that you killed a man," Liv said, rising to look into his face.

"The first one face to face."

"And your friend died?"

"Actually, no." the doctor replied, "at least not then. Preston was shipped home. I never heard from him again."

◆

Sean O'Malley lifted the top tray from his steamer trunk to pack his few belongings when he noticed the canvas-wrapped box. Setting his folded shirts down on the bed, he carefully lifted the bundle out of the trunk and placed it on the desk. Gently unwrapping the ancient container, he admired the top panel imagery again. The knight in the Templar tabard held the relic in both hands in a manner similar to the way one would hold a pistol. The energy that shot from it expanded out in a wedge.

The priest examined the worn part of the panel more closely. There was something there. The paint had worn away, but there were faint impressions in the wood itself. The image was a relief. He looked about frantically, finally settling on a water glass on the bathroom counter. Using it as a magnifier, O'Malley inspected the indentations. He could barely make them out. He needed to make them more distinct.

He knew that the archivists at the Vatican would admonish him for disturbing the relic, for the box was a relic in itself. But he needed to see what was hidden in the wood. He found a can of talcum powder in the bathroom and poured a liberal quantity on the worn section. Using his shaving brush, he then brushed away the excess, revealing the pattern beneath. The grayish-white powder not only exposed the worn section, but also enhanced the painted portion as well.

The knight did indeed hold the object, but it actually encased his left hand. The right hand rested on top of it. The beam from it spread wide to encompass numerous, previously-hidden figures facing the knight. They resembled insects in that they had bodies consisting of two segments, three pairs of legs, and dragonfly-like wings. The things varied in size, which O'Malley conjectured to indicate perspective; some were closer than others. All appeared to be caught in the beam.

Curious, he opened the box using the procedure the archbishop had shown him, and the top slid off. The strange device sat in a depression that time had worn in the box's faded, velvet lining. He used the glass to take a closer look without touching it. On closer inspection, the surface appeared to be more like a seashell than a gourd. The ripples and bumps were in a regular, uniform pattern. The surface was a dull, black color.

As his gaze wandered over the device, he noted that one end was rounded while the other was flatter. There was a small hole in one end, barely visible through the bottom of the glass on the flatter side, just where the object sank into the velvet. He moved in closer, and the hole expanded slightly! He recoiled, and when he looked back, it appeared to be the same size it had been originally. He moved closer again, and the diameter of the opening did increase perhaps an eighth of an inch.

He moved the glass to an inch or two away from the hole. The entire device widened until the hole looked big enough to insert his hand into it. O'Malley wavered for only a moment before picking up the device in his right hand and sliding his left hand into the opening. The object shrank until his hand was snugly encased. It was not heavy or painful, and there was a tingly feeling running from his fingertips up his arm.

Suddenly, there was a knock on his cabin door. O'Malley tensed, the energy running up his arm reversed, and a bolt burst from the other end, propelling the device into his face. The beam struck the canvas wrap of the box, and a three-inch area blackened and started to smoke. Thrusting the encumbered hand behind his back, he stepped to the door and opened it.

"Wire for you, Father," Mr. Moretti, the ship's communications officer, said with a salute. "Is something burning?" he asked, smelling the smoke.

"Everything is fine," O'Malley replied as he accepted the envelope. "Thank you, Mr. Moretti. Good night."

"And a pleasant evening to you, Father."

O'Malley closed the door after the man turned and walked away, making sure to lock it. He returned his gaze to his left hand. There were no marks or controls other than the rippled pattern on the surface. He experimented trying to push the segments apart with his free hand, but to no avail.

The priest's heart was beating rapidly. He sat on the bed and took several deep breaths. Then he laid down, closed his eyes, and willed himself to relax. O'Malley sighed loudly when the pressure around his left hand diminished, and the object slid off onto the bed.

Relieved, he opened the envelope, which he had placed on the bed. The telegram was a reply to the one he had sent to Dr. Feldman's home announcing his imminent arrival in New York.

RYKOV AND LAMB IN NYC STOP MEETING WITH TEPLOW ABOUT LONGBOROUGH STOP WILL MEET SHIP STOP FELDMAN

O'Malley smiled. It would be good to see them again.

Chapter 14

July 13, 1929

Anna sat alone in the dark for what seemed like hours. There was no light, not even from under the door. Trapped in the chair, she had tried calling out, but there had been no response. Other than the occasional groan from the man in the wardrobe, there were no sounds at all. She reasoned that the room was deliberately soundproofed as she also heard no sounds from beyond the door.

Anna felt helpless clamped to the chair, but she was more annoyed than afraid. Her body was getting stiff from the lack of movement, and her throat was dry, but mentally she was alert and focused. She reasoned that it would be better not to upset her captors. Other than confining her, they had not mistreated her, and as long as she was not antagonistic, they did not seem inclined to hurt her. But they would probably not believe her story. She barely believed it herself.

The door opened and the woman in the red catsuit flipped on the light as she entered. She stepped behind Anna, grabbed her hair tightly, and pulled it until Anna was face to face with a large man in a grey suit looking down at her. From the woman's deference, Anna could tell that this man was clearly in charge.

"I think you will agree," he said, "that Rose has demonstrated the gravity of the situation." He glanced at the contents of Anna's wallet. "Wouldn't you, Miss Rykov?"

"Dr. Rykov," Anna said hoarsely through gritted teeth. "Who are you to imprison me with this sadist!"

"I beg your pardon, doc," the boss said with mock sincerity. Louie entered and closed the door behind him. Then, he pulled up a chair in front of Anna and the leader sat in it. The boss nodded to Louie, who handed him a glass with a straw in it. The boss held it toward Anna and said, "Have a drink."

From the wardrobe, desperate grunts were heard. Rose slapped the wardrobe hard with her riding crop and the noises abruptly stopped. Anna took a tentative sip. It was water. She took a more substantial drink.

"As for why I have left you in Rose's custody," the boss said. "I need to know who set up the hit on Wendell. On his birthday, no less."

"I don't know what you are talking about," Anna said flatly.

"My rivals claim to know nothing about it," he continued conversationally, ignoring Anna's comment, "so if there's a new player in town, I need to know all about him. Tell me voluntarily, or I'll have to resort to less-pleasant methods." He glanced at Rose, who sneered with a feral grin, and then he pulled the glass just out of reach.

There was a muffled cry from the wardrobe. All four of them turned toward the sound. Rose flipped a switch on its side. A red light appeared around the gaps in the door and the cry rose to a muted scream. Rose flipped the switch again, and the outburst drifted into a muffled whimper before subsiding altogether. The boss returned his gaze to Anna with an expectant expression.

"I was brought to that restaurant by Mr. Gulden," Anna replied with animosity. "He said he knew it, and that we had business to discuss." The boss's expression was unchanged. "I picked an interior seat to be out of the sun."

"What kind of business?" the seated man asked.

"He claimed to be a private investigator looking into the same missing person that my colleagues and I are trying to find. He suggested that we compare notes."

"Why did you pull a gat on him?" Louie asked, "if you was so close?"

"I did not say that we were close. In fact, I only met him this morning. It was quite unexpected when I ran into him this evening."

"And the gun?" the boss probed.

"He knew things about my colleagues and I that I had not disclosed to him and there was no way that he could have uncovered them in only a few hours."

"Maybe he got lucky," Louie said.

"They were not the kind of details one would document," Anna said. "They were more personal aspects that would not be publicly known." Rose and the Louie shared a knowing glance.

"Also," Anna continued, ignoring the innuendo, "when he introduced himself to us this morning, both of my colleagues had unconscious negative reactions to him."

"So, this 'unsettling' man approached you on the street and suggested having dinner?" the boss asked.

"Yes," Anna replied evenly, "that is correct."

"And he picked the place?"

"That is also correct."

"But you picked the table near my associates?"

"Yes," Anna said without emotion. "Gulden wanted to sit outside at first, and when I said I would rather be out of the sun, the waiter suggested a table that was still in direct sunlight. We sat at the only other available table."

"Where did you sit?"

"I sat with my back to the window."

"The fella wanted that seat and seemed put out with his back to us," Louie added.

The boss closed his eyes and rubbed his chin. Anna was about to speak when Rose glared at her. Finally, what seemed like minutes later, he opened his eyes again.

"Your date wanted you to face the window so the hit men would see you when they arrived. I suspect that you were the beard for his role in the hit." He looked Anna up and down. Rose licked her lips mockingly. "In fact, you were probably the marker." Anna's mouth gaped. "The shooters would spot a looker like you in a crowd easy and know to hit the guy you were with."

"What a cad," Louie said. "Using a dame for a target." He shook his head disapprovingly.

"Indeed," the boss said evenly. "Tell me about this Gulden fellow."

"His business card is in my purse." Louie rummaged through the bag and produced the card, which he handed to the boss.

"Peter Gulden with the Eastern Mutual Life Insurance Company." He handed the card back to Louie. "Check him out."

"Right, boss."

"Thank you for your assistance, Dr. Rykov," he said as he stood. "My associates are going to look into your story. In the meantime, you will remain here as my guest."

◆

Harry Lamb awoke with a smile to the smell of bacon. He rose from the pile of pillows and located the pantaloons. Then he followed the smell down the hall past the front door to the kitchen. Inside, the table had been laid out for two. Tea steeped in a porcelain teapot, and two matching cups on saucers sat next to it.

"Good morning," Liv Lee said with a broad smile. She wore a short, silk robe that clearly displayed she was naked underneath. She held two plates out, each bearing a piece of toast with a hole cut out of the center. Inside was a fried egg with the yolk side down. Several strips of nicely crisp bacon sat alongside. This was how Lamb's mother had made the eggs when he was a child. He had not had them like that since leaving home. "Just the way you like them."

He walked behind her, wrapped his arms around her waist, and reached inside the robe. She jerked to balance the plates as his kissed her repeatedly on the nape of her neck, while tenderly stroking her stomach with his fingertips. Just the way she liked it. She giggled.

"That tickles," she said with a laugh as she shuffled the two of them toward the table and put down the plates. She turned to face him and wrapped her arms around his neck for a passionate kiss. Then she let go, wormed herself free of his grasp, and sat down. "Time for breakfast."

"Where are we off to today?" Liv asked after daintily picking up a slice of bacon in two fingers, and then stuffing it in her mouth and sucking the grease from her fingers. Before Lamb could respond, she said, "I say we start with Frank. I may be able to worm something out of him." Lamb collected his thoughts.

"The first thing is to contact Anna. She should be back at the hotel," he corrected between bites. Liv gave an annoyed look for a moment. "We need to regroup. Where is your telephone?" She pointed to the front door.

"There's a phone in the lobby," she said matter of factly as she ate her eggs without emotion. Lamb noted her reticence, and took her hand. "There's still a job to do. We need to get to the bottom of this." She shrugged and kept eating.

"I'll be right back," he said, rising quickly.

"You might want to put some clothes on," she said absently. He examined himself and nodded. He returned to the front room where he had left his own clothes, closed the blinds, and dressed. As he was finishing, Lee came in and adjusted his tie. "Don't go without me."

Lamb nodded without looking and made haste out the front door and down the stairs, nearly colliding with an older man on the second floor landing. He apologized and found the telephone on a small table in a niche next to the apartment manager's office. As he picked up the receiver, the door opened.

"That phone is for residents only," the manager said, clamping on a cheap cigar. Lamb stammered to respond.

"It's OK, Lou," Liv said as she gracefully descended the stairs, "he's with me." Lou looked them both over.

"I bet he is," Lou said, closing the door behind him. "Tramp," Lamb heard in a muffled voice as it shut. Lamb turned and looked Liv over. She wore yellow trousers and a white vest under a wide-lapelled pale, green jacket. A large necklace of matching stones around her neck drew one's attention to her cleavage. The necklace seemed familiar to Lamb.

"Come on," she said impatiently, "we're losing daylight." Distractedly, Lamb flipped the switch on the telephone until a voice responded.

"Number, please," the operator said with an uninterested, nasal voice.

"Hotel Lexington, please," Lamb replied.

"Swanky," the operator said with amusement. "One moment please." There was a pause.

"Hotel Lexington, Miss Young speaking."

"Hello. This is Dr. Harold Lamb. Please connect me to my suite."

"Oh, Dr. Lamb," Miss Young said excitedly, "I'm so glad you called. Someone broke into your suite last night."

"Was anyone hurt?!"

"What happened?" Lee cried, sidling up beside him and placing her arm around his waist.

"No, Dr. Lamb. No one was there." There was a pause. "According to the night clerk, none of your party came and asked for the key. When will you be returning? The hotel detective wants you to inspect your belongings and see if anything is missing."

"I'm on my way," Lamb replied with urgency. He hung up the receiver. "Someone broke into our room last night," he said. "But I'm more concerned that Anna and Ganon did not return to the hotel. We'd better get over there and get a first-hand look," Lamb said and stepped purposely toward the street exit.

Chapter 15

July 13, 1929

"Hotel Lexington," the cabbie said as he pulled up to the curb. Lamb paid the driver as a red-coated doorman opened the door.

Lamb stepped out. Once clear, the doorman helped Liv out of the cab. They did not pause to tip the doorman. Instead they made haste through the front doors. The other occupants of the grand lobby made space for them and they headed straight for the front desk.

As they approached, the woman behind the counter that they were heading for waved someone over, who intercepted the trio short of the desk.

"Can I help you?" an expressionless man in a brown suit said, standing in their path.

"I'm Dr. Harry Lamb. I was told that my suite was broken into."

"I'm Bob Kirby," the man said, "the hotel detective."

"What happened here?" Lamb asked, refocusing the conversation.

"Let's go somewhere more private," Kirby said, gesturing toward a door at the end of the counter. After a pause, Liv started walking, and the others followed. Kirby stepped around them and opened the door to a small meeting room.

"Someone went through your suite last night," the detective said when all were seated around the table.

"Was anything taken?" Lamb asked.

"That's what we need you to determine, doctor. The place was pretty torn up. Pillows, cushions, mattresses. Drawers dumped, and so forth." Kirby looked directly at Lamb. "Can you think of any reason someone might have wanted to search your rooms?"

"I have no idea," Lamb replied. "We were all out all night."

"Shouldn't you be taking notes or something?" Liv said with a look of suspicion. "For that matter, how do we know you are who you say you are?"

"I can understand your reluctance, Miss…"

"Lee," she said at his prompt. "Miss Lee will do."

"Very well, Miss Lee." Kirby went to the door, opened it, and signaled to someone. A moment later, Mr. Lyons, the manager who had assisted them when they first arrived, appeared at the door looking anxious.

"You know Mr. Lyons, the night manager," Kirby said. Lamb nodded. "Mr. Lyons, please tell these guests who I am."

"Of course," Lyons said, nervously glancing at Kirby, "This is Mr. Kirby, the hotel detective." He turned to the others. "I want you to know how sorry I, and the Hotel Lexington, are that such an outrage could occur under our roof. Your accommodations and anything you need are on the house for the duration of your stay…"

"Unless you are somehow responsible for the incident," Kirby interjected. Lyons glanced back to Kirby.

"Of course," he said, then turned back to his guests. "It is hotel policy. As long as you are not responsible for the wrong doing, your stay will be at no charge."

"And that is what I have been charged with determining," Kirby added. "As long as the police don't need to be involved, you'll be OK. And even if they are, if you are merely the victims, you have nothing to worry about."

"Why would you suspect us?" Lamb asked with irritation. "We were only here one night, and we haven't been back since yesterday morning!"

"That's another thing," Kirby said, ignoring Lamb's question. "For the duration of the investigation, you will be the guests of the Hotel Lexington. We will, of course, provide another suite for you." He nodded to Lyons. "You may go now, Mr. Lyons." The night manager nodded to Kirby, smiled sheepishly at the others, and left the room wiping his brow with his handkerchief.

"Let's go upstairs and take a look at your suite, Dr. Lamb," the detective said, gesturing to the door. He smiled patronizingly at Liv. She returned the gesture. "If you need anything, Miss Lee, my man outside will summon Mr. Sutcliffe, the day manager." He turned to Lamb. "Shall we go?"

◆

Sean O'Malley stepped down the forward gangplank with his valise. A porter carried his steamer trunk on a hand truck. He scanned the assembled crowd awaiting the passengers, but did not see anyone he recognized. He wondered if Anna and Harry might be waiting at the aft gangplank, where the steerage and third class passengers debarked, but he dismissed the idea. Those people would be shuttled off to Ellis Island for customs and immigration. He and the other first and second class passengers had had onboard interviews with the port officials when the ship first docked.

"How long were you away, Father?" the young customs officer had asked, reading from the script on his clipboard.

"I was in Rome for two weeks," O'Malley replied, "and four days each way for the passage." The officer wrote the information down on the form.

"Do you have anything to declare?" he asked.

"No, my son," the father replied. "I was there on church business."

"That's a big trunk for a priest, isn't it?" He eyed O'Malley suspiciously. "Mind if I take a look?" O'Malley shrugged, unlatched the two closures, and opened the top. The officer flipped through the clothing on the top tray.

"Any problems?" O'Malley said.

"You have your clothing on the top tray," the officer replied. "Most people put it underneath. What are you hiding there?" O'Malley raised his eyebrows at the comment.

"Nothing at all," he said with a smile. "As I said, I was in Rome on church business. The bottom compartment is full of books and notes." And a priceless relic, he thought.

"Let me see," the officer commanded. O'Malley gave a deep sigh and carefully lifted the tray so as to not dump with neatly-folded clothes. He placed the tray on the bed. The officer pulled out a notebook and started flipping through it.

"Are you looking for anything in particular?" The officer gave him a skeptical look and pulled out another notebook. Then he noticed the canvas-wrapped bundle.

"What do we have here?" the officer said with feigned surprise. "Were you hiding this from me?"

"Not at all," O'Malley replied with indignation. "That is a holy relic that the Vatican has entrusted to me to deliver to Reister University. It is priceless and quite fragile, so I can't allow you to casually examine it." This pushed the young officer's officious attitude even further. He reached for the bundle, and O'Malley caught his hand.

"Young man," he said in a serious tone, emphasizing the first word, "if you insist on inspecting that bundle, I demand to speak to your supervisor." The young man was surprised, but before he could respond, O'Malley added, "If it must be disturbed, it will only be done so under proper, museum-quality conditions." He gave the officer his severe disappointed priest look. The officer gulped, glanced at his clipboard, and then looked to the father sheepishly.

"Um," he stammered, "if the article is so, uh, delicate…"

"It is," O'Malley pressed.

"If it is so delicate," he said with difficulty, "and a holy relic, as you say," O'Malley nodded, "then I suppose you have the authority to bring it into the country." He scribbled hastily on the form on his clipboard, tore off the bottom section, and handed it to the priest. "You are cleared to enter the country, Father." O'Malley lightened his expression.

"Thank you, my son," he said. He opened the cabin door. "I wish you a pleasant day." The officer took the hint and left the cabin. A porter was waiting by the door, and O'Malley gestured for him to come in. Then, he replaced the notebooks and the tray, closed the top, latched it shut, and locked it.

"Is that everything, Father?" the porter asked, looking about for other luggage.

"That is all," O'Malley replied. The porter looked surprised. "What is wrong?"

"Nothing, Father," he said. "It's just that first class passengers usually have a lot of luggage." He attempted to lift the chest. "Chri… Um, wow!," he said, correcting himself, "What do you have in there?"

"It's mostly books and notebooks," O'Malley replied. "I should have warned you."

"I'll be right back," the porter said as he left the cabin. He returned a few minutes later with a hand truck. He tethered the trunk to the hand truck with thick canvas straps and tested the load. "That should be OK. After you, Father."

◆

Kirby unlocked the door and stepped into the suite. Lamb followed and gasped. All the fine appointments had been destroyed. He immediately saw feathers strewn about the living room and tattered cushions thrown here and there. As they stepped farther in, he saw that the bottoms of the couches had been slit open.

"The whole place is like this," Kirby said. "Anything ring a bell?"

"I have no idea what they were looking for," Lamb replied, his hand covering his mouth in amazement. He strolled about the living room. "As I said downstairs, we had anything of value with us."

"Take a look around," the detective said from the doorway. "Maybe you'll remember something." Lamb did as instructed. He strolled slowly around the living room. Nothing had been left untouched, save for some lamps. The burglars probably needed the light. The coffee table they had had breakfast on was upside down. He noticed crumbs on the floor.

"Housekeeping has not touched the room," Kirby said, anticipating Lamb's question. "We didn't want to disturb anything until you had a chance to look around. Go ahead. Check out the bedrooms."

Lamb went into the room he had slept in. It was in a similar state. The bed was on its side, the mattress had been sliced open, his clothing had been strewn about the room, and the drawers of the wardrobe lay haphazardly on the floor. As he took inventory of his belongings, the detective appeared in the doorway.

"Anything missing?"

"I don't think so," the doctor replied. "I didn't bring much with me. We were only supposed to be here for a couple of days." He found his suitcase behind the bed. The lining had been sliced open. "Well, that's a loss," he said with frustration. He righted the bed and collected his clothing on it in neat piles.

"Perhaps they were after something Dr. Rykov had." Kirby gestured for them to leave the room and Lamb complied, unsure if it was a suggestion or a command.

"Anna kept most of her things in her purse." As they approached the door to the other bedroom, he added, "All she had aside from that was her suitcase."

"Let's see what we can find," Kirby said, opening the door and gesturing for Lamb to enter. That room was also a mess, though whoever searched here was more careful. The furniture was upright, but the mattress, and all the cushions and pillows, had been sliced open. The drawers were open, and Anna's clothing had been rummaged through. From the slant of some of the drawers, they had clearly been pulled out and replaced.

"Well this burglar was much more respectful," the detective said with a skeptical look. "Perhaps Dr. Rykov had something to do with it?"

"I don't know why she would want people to destroy our suite," Lamb said distractedly. Where was Anna? He last saw her yesterday afternoon, and they had not parted on the best terms. "Nothing seems to be missing," he concluded.

"So they either found what they were looking for or gave up."

"Maybe they were after something that dancer left behind," Lamb suggested. "Marylin Miller." Kirby paused and considered it.

"That's a possibility," the detective said. "She was pretty careless. Had the whole housekeeping staff up here searching for a necklace that she was wearing once." He nodded. "Good chance they were looking for something she left behind." Kirby took a breath. "But that doesn't explain ripping up the cushions and such, or leaving Dr. Rykov's things alone."

"It suggests that the burglars had respect for Ms. Miller," Lamb said hurriedly. "That would suggest an admirer, rather than a random burglar."

"That fits," Kirby agreed after a moment. "I think we've seen all we need to here. Pack up your belongings. When your new accommodations are ready, I'll have your things moved there."

Chapter 16

July 13, 1929

The pier was crowded, and the father had to press through the crowd, followed by the porter, until they reached a clear space beyond the assembly.

"Do you want me to hail a cab for you?" the porter asked, setting the hand truck down.

"No, thank you, my son," O'Malley replied. "I am expecting some friends. They must be running late."

"Would you like to store your trunk while you wait?"

"I don't think that will be necessary. As you have seen, it would rather difficult for someone to run off with it." He looked around. "Perhaps you could set it down over by that bench." He indicated an unoccupied wooden bench against the terminal building that faced the ship. The porter nodded and wheeled the hand truck over. O'Malley followed and sat on the bench. The porter unloaded the trunk and left it on the ground at his side.

"Is there anything else you need, Father?" the porter asked expectantly.

"No, thank you," O'Malley said, handing the man a nickel. The porter smiled appreciatively, saluted, and walked off with the hand truck. O'Malley scanned the crowd for signs of Anna or Lamb, but it was impossible to pick individuals out from among the sea of people. He decided to wait where he was until the crowd thinned out.

◆

Anna sat alone in the dark again for several hours. All was quiet. Even the man in the wardrobe had settled down. Trapped in the chair in the soundless dark, she found the situation almost relaxing. Aside from the metal restraints that immobilized her head, arms, and legs, and the hard metal seat, she was rather comfortable. After a while, she let her mind wander and considered what she had discovered.

Brian Teplow was somehow at the heart of this. Or was he? He had had visions of her, Harry, and even Arthur Cophen, ten years before what he had seen had occurred. At first, Brian's visions seemed to be linked to the trauma of losing his father. But why then would he be replaced by Khan-Tral and Deb-Roh? Brian had clearly idolized his father.

Then there was the matter of Ganon and the Pointees. He had an old, worn image that was identical to a drawing Teplow had made years before. And the figures in it were clearly representations of Anna, Harry, and Arthur Cophen, as well as Ganon and this Lee woman. And they all had been on a mission to rescue Teb-Roh.... No that was wrong. Deb-Roh.

Of course, she thought, it was phonetic inversion. The names had consonant replacements. Deb-Roh was Brian

Teplow. D for T was common enough. As was R and L. Harry was Nab. No, Lamb was Nab. N for L and B for M. Noh-gof is what Ganon called her. That was a bit of a stretch, N for R was less common, but did occur. But G for K was not unusual…

She was blinded again when the door opened again. She saw the silhouette of Rose, who waited a moment before turning on the lights. She entered, followed by the man that had stood during the initial visit, and who held a glass of water with a straw in it. Rose looked at him petulantly. The man frowned.

"Drink up," the man said, but paused before placing the straw near her mouth, "but don't do nothing stupid, or the boss might let Rose have you." He moved the glass closer, and Anna emptied the glass. "You want some more?"

"No, thank you," Anna said emotionlessly.

"I'll be back in a minute with the boss," the man said as he turned to leave, glaring at Rose on the way out.

"Looks like you won over the boss," Rose said casually. "He must have some use for you," she turned to the wardrobe and yelled, "unlike some pieces of trash!" There were muffled pleas from within before she flipped the switch again. The red light lit up the spaces around the door and the man cried out. She flipped the switch back and opened the little hatch. The makeup was smeared by his tears and drool hung from the corners of his mouth and from the gag.

"What did he do to deserve this?" Anna asked, matching the dominatrix's tone. Rose thought for a moment, glanced at the open door to the wardrobe, then to the open door of the room, and disappeared behind Anna.

"He slept with his daddy's mistress," she whispered in Anna's ear with a snicker, "and he was good. Now she doesn't know which one to choose."

"Why choose either…" Anna whispered back, but was cut off when Rose slapped the back of her head.

"Who asked for your opinion?" she snapped as the man in the gray suit entered the room.

◆

Lamb gathered up his belongings to place them in a laundry bin provided by Mr. Sutcliffe in light of the destruction of their luggage. Liv packed Anna's possessions, inspecting them as she neatly folded and placed them into another bin.

"A bit conservative for my taste," she said loud enough for Lamb to hear from the main room. She could see him through the open doorway, "but that just means more guys for me." Lamb did not react. "Her things would be too tight and short on me anyway." Again, nothing from Lamb. She knew what he was thinking about.

"I'm worried about Anna," he said, absently picking up yesterday's newspaper.

"She's a tough cookie," Liv said, emerging from Anna's bedroom. She took Lamb's arm and looked softly into his face.

"You really care about her?" she said. She was both moved and jealous of the doctor's devotion to Anna.

"We're just friends," Lamb replied, recognizing her concern. "We've been through a lot together." She scrutinized his face for a moment and her expression brightened.

The gathering on the pier had disbursed, and there was still no sign of Anna or Lamb. O'Malley considered his options. He could seek hospice accommodations at a nearby church. But that would impose on his fellow clergy and, in light of the peculiar circumstances of the past few weeks, might pull them into the strange happenings that seem to have ensnared him.

After waiting for almost two hours, he decided to send a telegram to Dr. Feldman and wait for a reply. Perhaps he knew where the others were staying. He flagged down a passing porter.

"Excuse me," he said, "can you direct me to the Western Union office?"

"Of course, Father." The porter pointed to the nearest doors. "It's inside to the right about halfway down." He noticed the trunk. "Do you need me to move that for you?"

"Yes, thank you." The porter tried to lift the trunk and cursed under his breath. "I should have mentioned," O'Malley said apologetically, "it's full of books."

"I'll be right back," the porter said and ran off into the terminal. He returned a few minutes later with a hand truck. He tethered the trunk to the hand truck with the canvas straps as the other porter had on the ship. "This way, Father."

O'Malley followed the porter to the Western Union office. There was a line at the counter waiting for an open window, and several people huddled around the table with the forms. The porter waded into the crowd and returned with some forms and a pencil.

"Here you are, Father," he said, handing them to him. "You can use your trunk as a table." O'Malley smiled and started writing his message. The porter cleared his throat loudly. "Where would you like me to put it?"

"If you could wait while I send my telegram, I would appreciate it." O'Malley handed the man a dime. The porter tipped his hat and parked the hand truck. O'Malley composed his message and joined the line to send it.

At the counter, he handed the form to the clerk, who looked it over.

DR. ELIEZER FELDMAN

REISTER UNIVERSITY LIBRARY

WELLERSBURG

ARRIVED NEW YORK STOP NO ONE MET SHIP STOP WHERE ARE RYKOV AND LAMB STAYING STOP AWAITING REPLY STOP

FATHER SEAN O'MALLEY

"This is a long message," the clerk said through his chewing gum. "It's going to be expensive, Father."

"It's important, my son," O'Malley replied. The clerk shrugged and consulted his rate chart.

"That'll be sixty cents, then." O'Malley handed him the coins. "Thank you, Father. I'll send a runner when your reply comes. I suggest waiting in the cafe across the lobby." He noticed the porter with the trunk. "You can leave your trunk inside the door there," he indicated an area to the left of the door where other luggage had been deposited. "It'll be safe."

"Thank you," O'Malley replied with a smile. The clerk whistled and the porter moved the trunk to the storage area and unloaded the hand truck. Apparently this was a common practice. He crossed to the suggested cafe and ordered a cup of coffee while he waited for the reply.

He had had three cups and two slices of apple pie before a boy in a Western Union uniform appeared at his side.

"Are you Father Sean O'Malley?"

"I am."

"Telegram, Father." The boy handed O'Malley the paper. The father gave him a nickel and the boy ran off.

RETURN FOR FATHER SEAN O'MALLEY

AT HOTEL LEXINGTON STOP NO WORD SINCE YESTERDAY AM STOP WERE GOING TO FRANK AGENCY NEXT STOP

FELDMAN

They were staying at the Hotel Lexington. O'Malley decided to secure his trunk there. Summoning another porter, he had the trunk brought to the curb, where a taxi was waiting to take him to Midtown.

Chapter 17

July 13, 1929

When Lamb and Liv emerged from the elevator in the lobby, it seemed that everyone was reading the newspaper. Then they saw the headline: "TEN KILLED IN SHOOTOUT AT RESTAURANT."

Lamb's eyes widened. Liv snatched the paper from a man standing nearby and scanned the article, ignoring the man's protests.

"It says here that the dead were all members of Mickey Elder's gang," she said. "The restaurant is around the corner."

"Maybe Anna was there!" Lamb cried.

She handed the newspaper back to the man. "Let's go," she said confidently as she turned and headed to the front desk. Lamb followed.

Liv handed the key to the woman behind the counter

"The first step is to talk to the cops," Liv said when Lamb caught up with her. She took his arm and started toward the door.

"Do you think that's wise?" Lamb asked. "We can't explain ourselves in a way any rational man would believe."

"Don't worry," Liv said "If Anna was hurt, they'll know where she is now."

◆

With the practiced expertise of a native, Liv navigated down the crowded sidewalk. Lamb struggled to keep up with her. He caught her when she stopped at a stop light and took her arm. She embraced him and smiled. When the light changed, Liv continued at her accelerated pace and it was all Lamb could do to keep up with her.

When they approached 43rd Street, the crowds thickened. Again, Liv advanced through the mass of people effortlessly. When they rounded the corner, they saw that 43rd Street, which was a narrow, one-way street, had been closed to traffic. There were several police cars parked in the street, and a large crowd of officers conferring in front of a row of shattered windows.

"Miss Lee," a voice said from behind them, "what brings you to a crime scene? And who is this fellow? Given up on Brian Teplow?" Lamb turned to see the man he and Anna had shooed away outside Liv's apartment, pad and pencil in hand. "Where's your lady friend, Mr.?"

"Dr. Lamb is an old friend of mine," Liv interjected before Lamb could respond. "He heard of my despair and came to console me." She patted his arm and smiled in a sisterly manner. "He suggested that we get out of the apartment since it seemed that you jackals had finally run off, and we were attracted by the crowds like everyone else."

"Can you tell us what happened here?" Lamb asked. "The *Herald* was rather vague." The reporter scrutinized Lamb's face for a moment and said, "What's it worth to you?"

"It's worth an exclusive with Brian," Liv replied. "Once he is found and up to it, of course." The reporter tapped his pencil on his lips a few times, clearly considering it.

"OK," he finally said. "That's the spot where the shootout was. Seems that some of the Elder gang was celebrating Wally Elder's birthday."

"Wendell Elder," Liv corrected him.

"You know him?" the reporter queried.

"I may have met him once or twice at the theater," she replied coyly. Lamb was astonished at her candor. The reporter smirked.

"Well, Elder and his goons were celebrating in the back when these two guys with choppers came in and shot up the place. Six of the Elder gang, including Wendell, and four other folks were killed, and a dozen other people were injured."

"Do you know who was killed?"

"What's it to you?"

"We're looking for my colleague," Lamb responded automatically. "The woman I was with when we, uh, met, yesterday. She didn't return to our hotel last night and we thought she might have been here." Liv glared at Lamb for letting his tongue wag.

"Do you know who was killed or who was taken to the hospital?" Liv said with irritation.

"The cops haven't released the names of the dead," the reporter replied. Lamb and Liv looked at him skeptically. "Wendell's a known commodity," he replied defensively, and then added, "but the injured were taken to Belleview."

"Thank you," Lamb said. He turned to Liv. "Let's see if she's there." Then he steered her back toward Lexington Avenue.

"I'll be back for that exclusive," the reporter shouted behind them as they walked away. "The names Winchell, Walter Winchell, with the *New York Herald.* I know where you live."

◆

"It appears that you have been telling me the truth, Anna." The boss smiled patronizingly. "May I call you Anna?" He did not wait for a reply. He started looking at the various whips, knives, and other unpleasant devices hanging from the walls.

"My people went through your rooms at the Hotel Lexington," he said, stopping to admire a large knife with a long, curved blade.

"Nice place." He moved on to a branding iron hanging from a thong and held it up so Anna could see the design. It was a symbol she had seen before.

"They didn't find anything linking you to anything." He removed it from the hook along with a small, rubber-headed mallet and nodded. Rose slowly undid the top few buttons of Anna's blouse. "But you could have covered your tracks." He slowly moved toward Anna. The design was familiar, but she could not place it.

"Is there anything you might have remembered since our last chat?"

Anna squirmed as he placed the grid against her chest. She gasped as he hit the end of the handle once with the mallet.

"I told you everything," Anna said nervously with. The man pulled the branding iron away. It stuck to her sweaty skin and left an imprint of the design in her flesh. Rose nodded appreciatively. The man sat in the chair he had used before and placed the implement across his lap where Anna could see it.

"We found some curious things in your purse," the man said, holding out his hand to the other man standing behind him. Anna's purse was placed into it. "Us guys always wonder what you dames keep in these things," he said with a grin. He removed Brian Teplow's sketchbook and flipped through the pages. "Tell me about this."

"That belongs to the man we are looking for," Anna said. "He disappeared a few weeks ago, and the police have no leads. My colleagues and I were exploring his mental state before the disappearance in hopes of finding some clues." The man nodded.

"What's so special about this guy?"

"He's a spirit medium," Anna said. "His name is Brian Teplow. You may have heard of him." At the mention of the name, Anna saw a hastily-concealed look of surprise. "The police have no leads, and his mother is very worried."

"And what does this have to do with an upstate college professor?" he said the world slowly, as if struggling with each syllable, "from a university out in the country?"

"As I said," Anna replied, "we are looking into aspects that the police may have overlooked."

The seated man looked pensive for a moment. He held up the branding iron and examined the design absently. Anna finally recognized it. "Where did you get that device?" The man was surprised by the question.

"What's it matter to you?" he said.

"I have seen that design before," she said, "and not under favorable circumstances." The man was intrigued.

"Perhaps you should tell me about that."

Chapter 18

July 13, 1929

The doorman opened the doors for Father Sean O'Malley and he passed through, followed by a porter hauling his trunk on a luggage cart. He walked up to the front desk and was greeted with a smile by a well-groomed man.

"May I help you, Father?"

"Please call up to my friends' rooms and let them know that Father O'Malley has arrived."

"Of course, Father," the man replied, "and who are your friends?"

"Dr. Anna Rykov and Dr. Harold Lamb." At that, the man's face soured. He looked from side to side until he saw someone.

"Just a moment, please," he said, before walking swiftly over to a man in a brown suit. After a brief exchange, the two returned. The man in the brown suit walked up to O'Malley and held out his hand.

"Good afternoon, Father," the man said, "I'm Bob Kirby, the hotel detective. Can we speak in private?" He gestured toward a door at the end of the reception desk.

"Is there some problem?" O'Malley inquired.

"There was an incident," Kirby replied. "It would be better to discuss it in private." He gestured again. "This way, Father."

O'Malley signaled the porter to follow him and proceeded to the opened door.

"You can leave that there, Johnson," Kirby said to the porter. Johnson sighed, deposited the trunk on the luggage cart just inside the door, and left the room. Kirby closed the door.

"Please have a seat," he said, indicating the comfortable-looking chairs around a conference table. When O'Malley was seated, he said, "Your friends' suite was broken into and ransacked last night, Father."

"Were they hurt?" O'Malley asked anxiously as he stood.

"They're fine," Kirby replied. "They were out all night. We are making arrangements for other accommodations for them, but they did not mention that you were coming."

"My ship just arrived this morning," O'Malley said after taking a calming breath and sitting down again. "I had expected them to meet me at the pier."

"Well, neither Dr. Rykov, Dr. Lamb, or Major Ganon came back to the hotel last night." Kirby noted O'Malley's expression when he mentioned Ganon. "You don't know Major Ganon?"

"I've never heard of him," O'Malley replied, "but Dr. Rykov is from the city and probably knows a lot of people here." Kirby was satisfied with that response. "Where are they now?"

"Dr. Lamb was here about an hour ago. He and Miss Lee gathered up their belongings to transfer to the new rooms when they are available. Will you be needing accommodations, Father?"

"I expect so. We were to return to Reister University together. Do you know where they went?"

"They didn't say. Perhaps the girls at the desk heard something when they returned the key?"

"No," O'Malley responded, "that won't be necessary. I think I know where they have gone." He looked at his trunk. "I need to put my baggage in the hotel safe."

"That won't fit in the safe without blocking access to some safe deposit boxes," Kirby replied. "Do you need the whole trunk secured? We can store it in the luggage room for you." O'Malley thought for a moment.

"Perhaps you can accommodate my cargo," he said, standing and approaching the trunk. "I have a holy relic that the Vatican has entrusted me to deliver to Reister University." He unlocked the trunk.

"What kind of relic?" O'Malley opened the trunk. He removed the tray with his clothes and placed it on the conference table. Then, he uncovered the canvas-wrapped bundle and carefully removed it.

"This box dates from the Middle Ages and its contents are even older," O'Malley said in a serious tone. "It is going to the university for study. Dr. Rykov is an anthropologist." Kirby nodded understanding. "Will your safe accommodate this?"

"May I?" Kirby said, approaching the box. O'Malley nodded. Kirby made a rough estimate of the dimensions using finger spans. "I think this will fit in one of the larger boxes. Let me see if there is one available. I'll be right back."

O'Malley replaced the clothing tray inside the trunk and closed the lid. When Kirby had left the room, O'Malley put his valise on the table, opened it, and inspected the contents. In addition to the relic, the archbishop had provided him with some other tools. He removed some notebooks from the top to reveal a pair of wooden boxes. One box was on its side and the other box filled the rest of the case. He glanced toward the open door and shielded the valise from view with his body.

Lifting the top off the larger box, O'Malley inspected the three racks of stoppered vials it contained. The corks were painted different colors, one red, one blue, and one green, and each held 24 stoppered vials Satisfied that none had leaked in transit, he restored the top to the box. Then, he removed the sideways box, unlatched it, and flipped open the top to reveal a Beretta Model 1923 automatic pistol, two loaded magazines, and a new box of 9mm ammunition. He closed and latched the box as Kirby returned. He returned the box to the valise before turning to the detective.

"Is everything OK, Father?" Kirby asked suspiciously.

"Yes," O'Malley replied smoothly. "Just looking over my papers to make sure I have the correct materials with me." He put the notebooks back in the valise and closed it. Kirby did not react.

"Your parcel will fit in an available safe deposit box, so we can secure it in the safe and store your trunk in the luggage room for you."

"Thank you, Mr. Kirby." The detective reached for the bundle, but O'Malley interposed. "If you don't mind, I would prefer to handle the parcel myself." He made an exaggerated display of carefully picking up the box, placing his hands on thicker folds of the canvas.

"Of course, Father," Kirby said. "This way." Kirby led O'Malley out the door and opened the counter to allow him to pass behind it. The staff at the counter made room for them to pass to a door that the suited man opened for them. In the room beyond was a vault. The suited man dialed the combination to open the safe, pulled open the door, and led the way to a large safe deposit box in the rear left of the vault.

"This box should accommodate your needs," the man said, turning the key in the lock and opening the door to the box.

"Thank you, Mr. Sutcliffe," Kirby said, holding out his hand. Sutcliffe handed him the key and left the vault. "This will be your key, Father. The only other key is kept by the manager on duty."

"That should be satisfactory," O'Malley said. Kirby held the safe deposit box door open. The box was larger than the parcel. O'Malley slid the bundle into it, inspecting it carefully before nodding to Kirby, who closed the door, locked it, and handed him the key.

"I'll see to your trunk," Kirby said as they exited the vault. Sutcliffe closed the door and turned the combination a few times as they left. "If there is anything else you need, Father, please see Mr. Sutcliffe."

"Thank you, Mr. Kirby," O'Malley said, walking casually but quickly toward the conference room where he left his luggage. "I'll just collect my valise and be on my way."

"If your friends return, would you like me to give them a message?"

"Just let them know that I have arrived and should be back for dinner." O'Malley offered his hand and Kirby took it. "Thank you again."

◆

Lamb was out the door before the taxi came to halt, leaving Liv to pay the driver. She hurried to catch up to him and met him as he passed through the doors. The waiting area immediately inside the door was crowded with a variety of sick and injured people, many speaking foreign languages. Lamb pushed his way past them to the desk.

"Excuse me, sir," the desk nurse said, "but you'll have to wait your turn."

"I'm Dr. Harold Lamb," he said with authority, "I'm looking for a possible victim of the restaurant shooting last night." The nurse responded automatically and checked a clipboard hanging on the wall behind her. "Her name is Anna Rykov."

"I don't see that name here, Dr. Lamb," the nurse replied, "but several people were brought in unconscious or unable to communicate. You should speak to the duty nurse on the 3rd floor." She indicated the elevators to her left. Lamb immediately turned to them.

"Thank you," Liv said before following him. She arrived as the doors opened. They waited for some people to step out before entering along with a few others.

When the door opened on the third floor, Lamb stepped purposely up to the duty nurse's desk. Staff and patients moved out of his way. The large woman did not look up.

"I'm Dr. Harold Lamb," he said with authority. "I'm looking for…"

"Just a moment, doctor," the nurse said, writing something on a form. When she finished, the nurse looked up. Now," she said with a professional smile, "how can I help you?"

"I'm looking for a woman who was brought in after that shooting last night. The nurse downstairs said that there were several unidentified patients."

"Of course, doctor." The nurse pulled a list from under a pile of papers. "All of the patients have since been identified, Dr. Lamb. Who are you looking for?"

"Dr. Anna Rykov," he replied. She glanced at the list.

"There's no one listed here by that name."

"A short brunette? Scars on the left side of her face?"

"I'm sorry, doctor," the nurse said with a shrug. Another nurse emerged from a room behind the desk.

"Did you say you were looking for someone from the restaurant shooting named Anna?" the new arrival asked.

"Yes," Lamb replied with urgency. "Do you know where she is?"

"No, sir," the nurse replied, "but another fellow with a head wound was brought in mumbling something about someone named Anna being taken by the wizard, or something like that." Lamb looked around.

"Do you know his name?" Lamb interrogated.

"Was it Ganon?" Liv asked more politely. "A Major Ganon?"

"I don't recall him giving a name," the nurse replied, "but he was pretty beat up. He was taken to the Psych ward after his head was cleaned up."

"That's on the tenth floor, Dr. Lamb," the duty nurse added. Lamb turned on his heel and stepped up to the elevator. Liv smiled at the nurse and joined Lamb at the elevator as he pressed the up button.

Chapter 19

July 13, 1929

O'Malley emerged from the elevator onto the 14th floor of the building housing the Frank Theatrical Agency. A crowd of people milled about in the hallway waiting in front of the various offices. O'Malley waded through them, glancing at the names stenciled on the windows of the various offices until he reached the end of the hall.

The window in the door of the last office on the left was shattered. Inside, the room was in shambles. Every drawer in the numerous filing cabinets and the desk had been dumped on the floor, and a matronly woman with her back to the hallway was on her knees organizing the scattered papers. At the rear of the room was a door to another office that was also in disarray.

O'Malley knocked on the door frame. The woman jumped at the sound.

"As you can see," the woman said with irritation, continuing with her organizing, "we are not in any condition to see people today. If you had an appointment with Mr. Frank, he's not here anyway."

"Excuse me, miss," O'Malley said politely. 'I'm Father Sean O'Malley." The woman glanced at the priest, and immediately stood and smoothed out her dress with unconscious humility.

"I'm sorry, Father," the woman said humbly. "Someone broke into the office last night and, as you can see, they made quite a mess of things."

"I was looking for some friends of mine who were coming to see Mr. Frank," O'Malley said calmly, trying to put the woman at ease. "I was hoping to meet up with them here." She appeared to be holding back tears. He looked about the office and said, "Perhaps I can be of some assistance."

"That would be very kind, Father," the woman replied, "but I couldn't impose on you."

"Nonsense. I would be happy to help, and perhaps my colleagues will show up after a while." The woman wavered. "I have no other ideas where to look for them," he added with a smile. The woman shrugged.

"OK, Father," she said with a politely. "My name is Agnes Rasmussen," she said restoring her name plate to the desktop. "Mr. Frank' secretary."

"Pleased to meet you, Agnes." O'Malley stooped to start gathering the papers, but Agnes stopped him.

"The mess in here needs to be reviewed and sorted," she said. "I'd better do that myself." She glanced into the other room, hesitated, considered the priest, and then said, "but I suppose you could clean up Mr. Frank' office, Father." She indicated the inner door. "It will take days for me to make sense of all this."

"Very well," O'Malley said and stepped carefully among the papers through the doorway. The inner office had a view of 53rd Street and the building across the street. Two chairs lay on their backs in front of the desk before the windows. The desk chair lay on the floor to the right, with a bookcase leaning precariously on top of it. Its contents were strewn all over the floor.

He put his valise on the desk and righted the trash can. He used some of the waste papers to shovel the garbage back into it. Among the refuse, he found a business card for a Peter Gulden of the Eastern Mutual Life Insurance Company. On the back of the card was written "About the Brian Teplow matter. Urgent." O'Malley put the card in his pocket.

As with the outer office, two of the drawers of the desk had been pulled out and dumped. The bottom drawer was still in place. O'Malley tried to open the drawer, but it was firmly stuck. He stood the bookcase up to reveal a pile of leather-bound books and some sculptures and statuettes. He picked up the nearest, which bore a female angel with spread wings and a brass plate inscribed with "Molly's Folly, 1923." He placed it on one of the shelves and picked up another piece. It was a ceramic turtle, perhaps of Chinese origin, and when he lifted it, a panel fell out of the bottom along with a ring with two keys.

O'Malley picked up the keys and the panel. One of the keys bore a tag labelled "B.T." The other was not labeled. He examined the bottom of the sculpture and saw that the missing piece slid into the gap, but the tongue that would hold it in place had broken off. He put the piece into the slot and placed the sculpture next to the trophy. He picked up and examined several other trophies and sculptures, but found nothing of interest. Next, he replaced the books, which were all leather-bound copies of Shakespeare plays, and placed them on the shelf alphabetically.

When he had cleared the space in front of the bookcase of books and artwork, he started collecting the assorted papers, glancing casually at some as he gathered them together and placed them in piles on top of the desk. Many of them were bills marked "PAST DUE." Among them he found a cream-colored page of stationary. He pulled it out to find a neatly-handwritten letter addressed to Frank on Cavalier Club stationery.

You are now one month late with your payment for the services my associates rendered to you. If I do not receive payment in full by midnight on Friday, I will assign my collection agents to help you make good on your debt. Please remit at your earliest convenience.

M. Elder.

O'Malley folded the page and put it into his pocket.

"Any trouble, Father?" Agnes said, ducking her head into the office. She noted the papers on the desktop that O'Malley was trying to sort and said, "Don't worry about that, Father. Just get them up off the floor. I'll sort through them later" He noted the hint of apprehension in her voice, nodded, and smiled disarmingly. He returned to the papers on the floor.

When he had cleared the area in front of the bookcase he started working on the mess behind the desk. He attempted to insert the second drawer, but the stuck bottom drawer interfered with its insertion. He examined the space in the desk for the second drawer more closely and noticed that the panel between the second and third drawers had come loose and was wedged between the track of the third drawer and the drawer itself. He slowly worked the third drawer back and forth until a gap appeared, and eventually he pried the panel free with a wooden ruler.

The bottom drawer slid open. Inside was a stack of papers. He could still hear Agnes in the outer office. As quietly as he could, O'Malley flipped through the contents of the drawer. There were several insurance policies stacked there. He found one for Brian Teplow and pulled it out. It was from the Metropolitan New York Life Insurance Company for $500,000, and named Frank as the sole beneficiary. He returned the documents to the drawer, placing the Teplow policy on top, stood, and walked over to the dividing door.

"From what I've seen, Agnes," he said with his judgmental priest voice, "it seems that Mr. Frank is in a bit of financial trouble." Agnes glanced toward the windowless outer door, and then gently pushed O'Malley into the inner office.

"Don't need to let the world know," she said in a whisper. She glanced at the stacks of bills on the desk, and then noticed the insurance policy in the open bottom drawer. She scanned the document, and when she saw the amount, her jaw dropped. "Woody loved Brian." She looked at O'Malley. "Surely you're not thinking he did something to harm the boy?" She shook her head emphatically. "He wouldn't do such a thing. He couldn't."

"When is Mr. Frank expected?" Agnes sat on the desktop, knocking a pile of papers back onto the floor, and put her head in her hands.

"He hasn't been back since lunchtime yesterday," she said through quiet sobs. "He left here all upset and said he would be back later. But he hasn't come back since. I called his apartment several times, but there was no answer. I figured he was trying to get another loan to hold off the creditors."

"How long has he been struggling?" O'Malley asked, lifting her chin and dabbing her eyes with his handkerchief.

"Ever since Brian Teplow disappeared," she replied, regaining some composure. "Everything was fine for a couple of days, but after a week, it started to show on him. He got anxious, angry, started losing his temper for the smallest slight…" She started sobbing again.

"Why was Brian's disappearance so devastating? Surely Frank has a number of clients." Agnes shook her head.

"Brian was the cash cow," she said. "He was the real deal. Sure, Woody has some actors and vaudeville performers, but Brian generated more than the rest combined. And Woody had been increasingly neglecting the other talent in favor of Brian. In the end, I was the one really managing the others."

"How long has Brian been missing?"

"Where have you been, Father? Brian's been front page news for weeks."

"I just got back from Rome this morning."

"Please forgive me, Father. I didn't mean to be so rude."

"Not at all, Agnes," O'Malley said with a smile. "You are under a great strain." He grew serious again. "Now, I found these keys. Where does Mr. Frank live? I'll go over there and see if he is all right."

"He lives on First Avenue at 38th Street," she said. "On the 12th floor."

"Very well," O'Malley said, picking up his valise. "I will go to his apartment and let you know what I find there." Agnes smiled with an expression of relief.

◆

"That device is a symbol of evil," Anna said emphatically. "It represents an entity that seeks to destroy humanity. You have been holding it sideways." The boss turned the brand toward himself and turned it first one way and then the other. Louis peered over his shoulder.

"I've seen that before," Louis said."

"Where did you see it?" Anna asked with urgency.

"We saw papers with that on it at Gulden's place," he finally said. "They were handouts for some church." Rose stepped around Anna to look at the symbol.

"Yeah," Rose said, "there was an ad for that church in yesterday's paper."

"The Church of Cosmic Understanding," Anna said. "It was on the same page as the article about Woody Frank." Louis was startled by the mention of the name. He ran out of the room. "You people had something to do with Brian Teplow's disappearance."

"You are here to answer questions," the boss said calmly. He glanced at Rose, who immediately slapped Anna's face. "Tell me why this church is dangerous."

"You would not understand," Anna replied. Rose moved to slap her again, but the boss grabbed Rose's hand.

"Why do you say that?" he asked.

"Most people do not accept the," Anna thought for the right words, "'otherworldly' elements of this case." The sitting man released Rose's wrist, but was otherwise impassive. "Unless you hear what I would tell you with an open mind, I fear that you will assume that I am lying…" She trailed off.

"I have yet to hear you say anything related to Wendell's murder," the boss said impassively. "I will be upset if you don't say something useful soon." He glanced to Rose. "And then things will not go well for you." Rose glanced at Anna and gestured agreement.

"Very well," Anna said with a sigh. "Take out the sketchbook in my purse." She waited as he did so. He opened it to the first page and laid it on his lap so Anna could see it.

"Very nicely drawn," he said appreciatively, "but what does this have to do with anything?"

"Those drawings were made by Brian Teplow ten years ago," Anna said. The man was about to speak as he flipped the pages until he saw images of Anna.

"How long have you known Teplow," he asked suspiciously.

"I have never met him," Anna replied. Rose was about to slap her, but the boss glanced at her and she lowered her hand.

"He seems to know you pretty well, based on these drawings." He continued to flip through the pages,

"I agree," Anna said. "And how could he do that without ever meeting me." She spied a drawing of the thing that attacked her in O'Malley's church. "Stop there," she said. He did so. "Look at my face." He looked at Anna.

"Yeah, so?"

"I do not have the scars on my face in the drawing," she said. "That creature made them."

"What creature?"

"That cloud materialized into a monster that attacked me. Flip the page." The next page showed the thing attached to Anna's face. Cophen's knife was flying toward it. "My colleagues managed to dispel it."

"You're saying that those scars were made ten years ago," Rose said with disbelief. "I know scars. Those are fresh."

"My scars are less than one month old," Anna said matter-of-factly. "Brian Teplow foresaw events that are happening now." The boss looked unimpressed. He flipped some more pages, stopping at the landscape Anna had seen in the subway.

"What is that?" he said with surprise, pointing at the giant, tentacle-faced creature.

"That is the entity that the symbol on your implement represents." He glanced at the branding iron and then the image. "You will notice similarities when the curved part is on the top." The man raised a hand for Anna to stop talking and closed his eyes for a moment. Then he closed the book.

"We looked into that Gulden guy, the insurance investigator," Louis said. "Turns out that there ain't no Eastern Mutual Life Insurance Company. And the address on that card is a flophouse on Delancey Street." The boss shook his head.

"So he deceived me too," Anna said angrily. "Why are you still keeping me here if I am a victim of this man?" Rose slapped Anna on the side of the head. The collar bit into her neck as her head jerked from the impact.

"Let's be civil here," the boss said. Anna was not sure if he was speaking to her or to Rose. "They found some interesting things at his place." He held up his hand, and a small, flat box made of a dark wood was placed into his hand. He put the box in his lap and opened it so Anna could see its contents.

"It seems our Mr. Gulden is a dope fiend," he said conversationally. Strapped into indentations inside the lid of the box were two old-fashioned, glass syringes. In the base of the box were two vials with cork stoppers containing a green liquid, and a few empty ones with a thick, muddy stain coating them.

"But we don't know what this is." He removed a vial, pulled out the cork, and winced as a bitter, acrid odor escaped. Anna's eyes started to water and she coughed violently, causing the collar to dig into her neck. The boss quickly replaced the cork and Rose reached from behind and put a wet handkerchief to Anna's face.

"Hush," the dominatrix said, and held the cloth firmly over Anna's eyes, nose, and mouth until she stopped struggling. When she removed the handkerchief, the boss was filling one of the syringes with the cloudy, brown fluid. Anna shuddered as she saw some of the green residue move slightly. Rose knelt to Anna's left and unbuttoned the cuff of the sleeve on Anna's blouse. "Don't squirm unless you have to."

Chapter 20

July 13, 1929

Lamb and Liv stepped off the elevator on the 10th floor. Unlike the 3rd floor, there was no waiting area. Immediately outside the elevator was an empty space, devoid of furniture or decoration. There was a windowless door on either side, and in front of each was a counter with a window that was covered with thick glass except for a space at the bottom for passing papers underneath. The dim, institutional lights in the ceiling gave the room a gloomy feel.

A large, muscular woman sat at the desk on the other side. She looked up from her paperwork when they stood before the window.

"May I help you?" she asked with a completely neutral demeanor.

"I'm Dr. Harold Lamb…" The woman held up a hand.

"Do you have identification?" She looked at Lamb pointedly. Lamb took his wallet from his jacket pocket and pulled out a calling card. He slid it under the window to the nurse. She took the card and inspected it. She looked at Liv. "And this is?"

"I am Liv Lee," she said with a smile. "You may have heard of me." The expression of the woman behind the glass did not change.

"What can I do for you, doctor?"

"We're looking for a man who was brought here last night after the shooting at the restaurant." The woman sat, motionless. "He was with another friend of ours who is now missing." Still no reaction. "Do you know who I am referring to?"

"Yes, doctor," she replied emotionlessly. "The patient is here." She pressed a button. "Please proceed to the door on my left." She motioned toward it with her head. The pair turned to go. "Not you, miss," the woman added. "Unless you have proof that you are a family member or authorized agent, only medical personnel are allowed access to the ward."

Liv looked around the empty room, but before she could speak, the woman said, "You may find it more comfortable to wait in the cafeteria on the second floor," and smiled briefly. Liv looked to Lamb. He shrugged.

"They have to be careful," Lamb said apologetically. "I'm sure a lot of people come here to break people out thinking their patient is here in error or without cause."

"Yeah, sure," Liv said resignedly. "I'll wait downstairs."

"We'll meet you there," he said, kissing her forehead. Then he pushed the button for the elevator.

"This way, please, Dr. Lamb," a large, muscular man in a white, orderly uniform said after opening a door from the 10th floor foyer. Lamb stepped through the door. Liv tried to follow, but the orderly blocked her with a meaty hand and said, "Sorry miss. Doctors only." Liv was distracted by the ding of the elevator arriving, and when she turned back, the door was closed.

The room beyond the door was a locker room. Rows of lockers lined the walls to either side. There was a bench in the center. The orderly pulled a ring of keys from his pocket and unlocked one of the lockers.

"Please put anything metallic or potentially edible in this locker, doctor," he said. "You will also need to remove your jacket, your tie, and your shoes."

"My shoes?" Lamb queried in surprise.

"Yes, doctor," the orderly replied. "Some of the patients are violent or self-destructive. We have to be careful not to provide them with anything they might harm themselves or others."

Lamb sighed and placed his jacket and shoes in the locker, followed by his wrist watch and the contents of his pockets. Then he removed his tie and hung it over his jacket on the hook.

"Is this satisfactory?" Lamb understood the precautions, but he was not amused. The orderly motioned for Lamb to turn. The doctor turned so the orderly could see his back.

"Yes," the orderly said when Lamb was again facing him, "Thank you. This way, please." They approached the door at the opposite end of the room, and the orderly knocked twice. The door was unlocked and opened from the other side.

Lamb looked to the orderly, who gestured for him to enter. The hallway beyond was long and straight. On either side were doors, equally spaced so that the doors to either side were not across from each other. Each door had a door near the floor and one at head height.

About halfway down the corridor, a small man with curly white hair in a lab coat held one of the small doors open and was looking into it. Another orderly stood nearby with a clipboard. After a moment, the small man closed the peephole door, nodded, and the orderly started writing as the man spoke.

Lamb followed his orderly down the hall to the other men. The other orderly leaned over and whispered into the short man's ear. Then both looked at Lamb.

"Dr. Lamb?" the short man asked holding out his hand, "I am Dr. Gabriel Faeber."

"Dr. Harold Lamb," he said, taking Faeber's hand.

"I understand you are here about the man who came in last night," Faeber said.

"Yes," Lamb replied, "that is correct. Major Ganon is a colleague of mine, and the last person that we know saw our friend, Dr. Anna Rykov, before the shooting last night."

"I see. That must be the Anna he kept telling us about," Faeber said without expression. "And you are aware of his fantasies about 'Pointees,' despotic wizards, and tentacle-faced giants?" He looked squarely at Lamb and peaked an eyebrow.

"Yes," Lamb replied with a sigh. "Major Ganon is suffering from shell shock. We served together in France. Lost most of his command at Soissons." Faeber's expression changed to one of compassion. "I've been looking after him when I can since we returned."

"I see," Faeber said again. "And do you believe that he poses no threat to himself or others?"

"Major Ganon is a broken man," Lamb said, "but he is no more dangerous than you or I."

"That is an interesting choice of words, Dr. Lamb," Faeber said, scrutinizing his face. Then he pointedly asked, "What is Major Ganon's first name?"

"Preston," Lamb replied without thinking. "Major Preston Ganon. May I see him now?"

"I don't see why not," Faeber said with unexpected cordiality.

"He's right over here," he added, gesturing toward a door on the opposite side of the hall. They stepped up to it, and Faeber opened the peephole in the door.

"Is this your Major Ganon?" Faeber stepped aside to let Lamb look inside. Ganon sat on a padded floor. The walls were also padded, with a high, barred window cut out. Ganon was wearing a green short-sleeved shirt and matching loose pajama-type pants. At the sound of the hatch opening, he looked up.

"Harry," Ganon said, standing and approaching the door. "Thank the gods you found me."

"Yes," Lamb said with a nod. "Yes, that is Major Ganon." He returned to the window. "Hello, Preston," he said with a subtle wink, "Are you alright?"

"I'm fine except for being locked up here!"

"May I speak with him face to face?" Lamb asked. Faeber nodded and the orderly with the clipboard approached the door.

"Step to the back of the cell, please," he said. Ganon complied and the orderly unlocked the door and opened it. Lamb stepped into the room and the door was closed and locked behind him.

"Five minutes, Dr. Lamb," Faeber said and turned away. The peephole closed before Lamb could say anything else. Lamb turned to shout, but Ganon grabbed his arm and pulled him down to the spongy floor.

"They can't hear anything out there," he said, patting Lamb on the shoulders.

"What happened? And where's Anna?"

"It was Khan-Tral," Ganon whispered to Lamb, "He's here and gunning for you!"

"What do you mean?"

"That Peter Gulden fellow is Khan-Tral." Ganon said with a wide-eyed nod. "He lured Anna to that restaurant and his goons shot it up! I got her out the back door, but somebody cold-cocked me. Next thing I know the cops bring me in. I told them what I had seen, and they locked me up here!" Lamb hushed Ganon when he started to get louder.

"We can't discuss that here," Lamb said conspiratorially. " We served together in France at Soissons. You are Major Preston…." He trailed off when he caught the vagrant's eye. "Carver? Is that you?" He put his hand in front of Ganon's mouth, concealing his moustache and beard, and gasped, wide-eyed. "It is you! It's me, Corporal Lamb!"

"Carver?" The vagrant seemed puzzled. "My name's Ganon."

"You said that you did not know your identity in the world," Lamb whispered. "But I know who you are. You are Major Preston Carver, my commanding officer during the War." The vagrant did not appear convinced. Lamb glanced toward the door.

"We'll tackle that later," Lamb said quietly. "For the time being, you are Major Preston Ganon. You are shell shocked. That means that your mind was unsettled by what you saw and your reality is askew." Ganon did not appear to understand. "Never mind. Just stick with that story and I'll get you out of here." Ganon nodded.

Suddenly, they heard the peephole door open and saw Dr. Faeber's face.

"Excuse my interruption, gentlemen," he said. Lamb detected slight anxiety in his voice. "Did you say you were looking for Dr. Anna Rykov?"

"That's correct," Lamb replied, the elation of his reunion with Carver gone. "She's been missing since the three of us parted company yesterday afternoon"

"It turns out that Dr. Rykov came to see me yesterday…"

"That's what I've been telling you," Ganon shouted.

"Yes," Faeber said with a nervous cough. "It appears that there is some validity to that part of your story." He nodded to his left. "With the information provided by Dr. Lamb, I have sufficient evidence to reevaluate your case."

The door was unlocked, and Faeber stepped inside. He walked up to Ganon and took hold of his wrist to take his pulse.

"What is your name?" Faeber asked expressionlessly, his gaze fixed on Ganon's face.

"My name's Ganon," he replied, but noticed Lamb's glance and added, "Major Preston Ganon."

"And how is it that you remember your full name now?"

"Seeing Corporal Lamb reminded me of when we first met in France." He shuddered for effect. Lamb put a hand to Ganon's shoulder to steady him.

Faeber scrutinized Ganon's expression, manner, and posture. After a moment he nodded and turned toward the door.

"A word, please, Dr. Lamb."

"I'll be back," Lamb said before following Faeber out of the cell. The orderly closed and locked the door.

"You have corroborated some of Mr... Major Ganon's story. His trauma is still severe, but I am willing to release him into your care, if you will answer some questions for me."

Chapter 21

July 13, 1929

Sean O'Malley gently pushed on the door to Woody Frank' apartment. He noted that it was ajar as he was about to knock, and he heard the sounds of a not-so-subtle search in progress. The rest of the floor was silent, but in the middle of the day in this part of town, he did not expect nosy neighbors. And clearly the person within did not either. He doubted the interloper would even notice his entrance.

To his surprise, while the door pushed open quietly, a glass containing a fine powder, which had been perched on the top of the door, toppled over. O'Malley was enveloped in the cloud of powder, and the glass fell to the hardwood floor with a clunk. The priest noticed movement within and spied a tall man looking towards the door with a hand reaching into his jacket.

Immediately to O'Malley's right was the open door to a closet, and he ducked into it moments before two shots struck the wall across the hallway. He crouched to the floor and fumbled in his valise with one hand while wiping the powder from his eyes with the other. He could hear the shooter mumbling something that sounded vaguely Scandinavian from.

O'Malley flipped open the wooden box and withdrew the small automatic and one of the magazines. He slapped the magazine into the pistol and chambered a round. Then he peered around the corner and saw the man gesturing wildly with his arms and spinning. The priest recognized the gestures as some kind of ritual magic from his training with Father Christophe, the Vatican authority on mystical things. O'Malley stepped from the closet and, holding the pistol in both hands, aimed at the man.

That is when the priest saw the top of a bloody head lolled back over the back of an easy chair. The gesticulating man was hovering over the body and periodically slapped the bloody man's head. O'Malley fired at the sorcerer and hit him in the throat and the chest. The man continued his incantation, now in a raspy gurgling voice, and then collapsed.

Suddenly O'Malley heard a buzzing sound, and subconsciously recognized it from when Anna was attacked at Dr. Lamb's house. Instantly, he fell to the floor and started fumbling through the valise again. He removed the wooden box and examined the three racks underneath it. O'Malley selected one each from the red and blue racks, as well as a large, silver crucifix, and crawled into the open area.

The numerous shallow cuts all over the chest and head of the man in the chair showed that he had been tortured. A pool of blood lay beneath him, and O'Malley had been fortunate enough not to step in it. However, the shooter had, and footprints led to a closed door, most likely to a bedroom.

The buzzing grew louder and O'Malley pulled the stoppers from both vials, ready to cast their contents on whatever came. Then he heard a rasping croak coming from the bloody man. He leaned toward the man and felt something swipe past his head. O'Malley turned and threw the contents of both vials in the direction the thing had come from. The particles seemed to combine in the air and coalesce to reveal the upper torso, head, and part of the arms of a giant, humanoid shape. The face was devoid of definition, other than two black pits where eyes would be, and a gaping maw that was equally empty.

O'Malley struck the giant with the silver crucifix, and the metal embedded in its cheek. The thing backhanded him with the invisible part of its arm, and the priest was flung across the room into the far wall, where he fell to the floor and was struck by a large mirror that had hung there. He looked up to see the entity pass through the intervening sofa. The crucifix slid through its face until it fell out from beneath its chin, leaving a gouge in its path.

O'Malley emptied the pistol directly into the thing. Each time, it was momentarily paused, but the bullets did not pass through it, and the monster seemed to be impaired slightly. When it reached for him, O'Malley flipped the heavy mirror up toward it and scrambled awkwardly toward the foyer and his valise. Not looking back, he reached into the bag and withdrew a vial from each of the three racks. He removed the stoppers from two before he was grabbed on the left side of his chest by powerful, sharp, invisible claws.

Reaching back, the priest cast the contents of the two open vials at the fiend. This time, the powders seemed to be attracted to the entity and clung to it, revealing more of its enormous form. O'Malley then grabbed the vial from the other hand and smashed it into the exposed thing. The vial was crushed on impact with the thick hide, sending shards into the priest's palm, but the monster immediately released him. It flailed, clawing at the now smoking spot where the vial had struck.

O'Malley drew another vial from each of the three racks, pulled the stoppers, and threw them all at the now more or less stationary entity. He hit it square in the chest and the vials shattered on impact. The monster emitted an almost inaudibly high wail, and disappeared into a cloud of foul-smelling smoke.

Panting, O'Malley examined his shoulder. The thing had pierced his cassock and undershirt, and both were sticky with blood. The wounds stung tremendously. He gingerly removed his cassock. Then he reached into the valise again and pulled a vial from the green rack. Removing the stopper, he was overcome by a powerful acidic odor. He winced involuntarily. Then he poured a small portion of the fluid on the gashes under his ribs. There was an instant of an intense, burning sensation, and then the stinging stopped. He then carefully poured the rest of the vial over the entirety of the wounds. He reached into the valise again, pulled out a roll of gauze, and wound it around his chest. He put the vial back into the valise and closed it.

Immediate needs met, O'Malley turned to the man in the chair. Lifeless eyes gazed back. The priest checked for a pulse, but found none. He considered trying the contents of a green vial on the bloody man, but opted against it. He was already dead. O'Malley search the man he had shot, whose lifeless face smiled broadly. The shooter's arms were covered with many years of needle marks, and O'Malley's bullet had pierced a curious symbol tattooed on his chest. O'Malley found some cash, a large, odd-shaped key, and several more of Peter Gulden's Eastern Mutual Life Insurance Company business cards. He put the key into his pocket.

O'Malley scanned the room. The living room had been rifled through, but as he peered through an open door he noted that that room had not been disturbed. Then he followed the bloody footprints and opened the door that they led to. The man had searched the bedroom. The drawers of the dresser had been pulled out and dumped. The bed had been tossed . The adjacent master bathroom had been tossed as well.

O'Malley could hear police sirens approaching. The neighbors must have called them. He went to the other room. It contained an old sea chest, a desk, and a closet. Inside the closet he found nothing of interest. As he searched the desk, a stack of papers caught his attention. They were paid bills from an Oak Valley Sanitarium in Chatham, New York, for the treatment of a patient named Daniel Meldon. He folded one, put it in his pocket, and closed the drawer.

The sirens had stopped. O'Malley ran quietly out to the foyer to collect his valise. He put the pistol back in the wooden box and closed it. As he put the box back into the valise, he heard the bell chime on the elevator and rapid footsteps approaching the still-open door. He grabbed the valise and made his way to the bedroom. He closed and locked the bedroom door. As he stepped out onto the fire escape, he heard sounds inside the apartment. Not stopping to listen, he quietly climbed the fire escape toward the roof, which was only two floors up.

The fire escape ended at the top floor. It did not ascend to the roof. The top landing stood before a large window into an apartment. The blinds were open, and O'Malley could see a maid preparing a meal in a kitchen. He knocked on the windows. The maid looked up and was about to scream when she appeared to recognize his cassock and collar. She ran to the window and opened it.

"What are you doing out here, Father?" she said in a lilting Irish accent.

"I stepped out onto the fire escape for some air," O'Malley improvised, "and the window closed on me. I tried as I might, but I couldn't open it from the outside. I tried all the floors, but no one was home. Praise the Lord that you were there, my child." The maid smiled at the comment and accepted his valise so that he could more easily climb through the kitchen window.

"Your coat is torn and bloody," she noted with concern.

"I caught it on the bars coming up."

"Well let me clean that off for you," she said, hurrying from the room. "Take off your shirt," she added from the hallway. O'Malley was about to sneak out when the woman returned with a washcloth and a bottle of iodine. "We need to clean that up or it will get infected," she said, unbuttoning the cassock. O'Malley stepped back.

"That is really not necessary, dear," he said firmly. "I'm on my way back to the rectory now. I promise I'll see to it when I get there." The maid looked disappointed, but nodded.

"As you please, Father," she said with a curtsy. O'Malley smiled, took the valise, and made his way quickly to the front door. He smiled again as he turned to open it, and stepped out into the hallway. There was a large mirror on the wall in the hallway, and he examined his appearance. He brushed the rust stains from his trousers and cassock and straightened his hair with his fingers. He gently felt the wounded area. The gauze was peeking out from the hole in his cassock. The wound was no longer sensitive to his touch. It would probably be scabbed over by the time he got to the Cavalier Club.

Chapter 22

July 13, 1929

"Dr. Rykov left a note yesterday concerning one of my old patients, Brian Teplow," Faeber said, guiding Lamb and Liv into his office and closing the door behind them. "Do you know the nature of the inquiry?"

"Dr. Rykov and I are investigating his disappearance on behalf of his mother," Lamb replied. "She corresponded with us when our associate at Reister University attempted to contact Brian about a meeting he had shortly before our previous client passed away."

"I see," Faeber replied. "If I may ask, who was your previous client?"

"Jason Longborough," Liv said, inserting herself into the conversation. "He asked Harry and Anna from his deathbed to perform a ritual to banish a demon," she said without hesitation. Lamb gave her a displeased glance. Then he turned to Faeber.

"And he spoke to Brian Teplow before this incident?" Faeber asked.

"He went to see Brian a few months ago," Lamb said after stopping Liv with a look. "His wife told us that he had been agitated and his health had been steadily declining, but after his meeting with Brian, his vigor seemed to have been restored."

"But it didn't last," Liv cut in. "He got news of one of his college chums passing away and fell ill again."

"Yes," Lamb asserted, taking control of the conversation again, "he seemed to relapse upon receiving that news and was hospitalized under my care. Despite our best efforts, he continued to decline, though there was no physical reason for it. So when Father O'Malley brought Anna to see him, and he asked her to do him a favor, I thought it might lift his spirits and his health might recover."

"There is data suggesting that a positive outlook promotes well-being," Faeber said. Then his demeanor changed. "But I take it the performance of this request didn't help," he added in a professional tone.

"We had not completed it before he passed," Lamb said with a look of despair. "But we did go through with it nonetheless."

"So why did Dr. Rykov want to see me?" Faeber's expression was neutral.

"Mrs. Teplow told us that you had treated Brian after both of his comatose episodes," Lamb said, glancing at Liv to prevent her interruption. "Since the police have no leads, we were pursuing other avenues of inquiry, such as his mental state before he disappeared. We thought there might be some clues in your notes."

"Tell him about the journals," Liv said excitedly. Lamb sighed.

"Brian kept journals in which he wrote stories," Lamb continued. "Childish fantasies at first, but after his father died the nature and tone of the stories changed."

"That is to be expected," Faeber said, nodding. "How did they change?"

"Well, I only read the journals prior to his first episode. Dr. Rykov read the ones written between the two. But she said that those stories featured two prominent characters, one a warrior and the other a small, quiet, sneaky type who chronicled their adventures. Anna believed the latter was Brian himself."

Faeber sat back in the chair behind his desk and steepled his hands before his face. He studied Lamb and Liv's faces several times. After a few moments he stood, produced a key from his pocket, and knelt down to unlock one of the lower drawers of the desk. When he rose again, he had two small notebooks in his hand. The covers were inscribed with "Teplow, Brian" and a range of dates corresponding to the periods of therapy following each of his extended hospitalizations. The more recent book had numerous scraps of folded paper among the pages.

"These are the notes from my two series of sessions with Brian under hypnosis," Faeber said in a serious, but more conversational tone. "They have been locked in that drawer since I last saw Brian three years ago." He sighed. "I haven't known what to do with them. I had considered writing a paper about Brian's condition, but with his subsequent fame, that struck me as unethical.

"As you described in the later journals," Faeber continued, "in the sessions after his first seizure, Brian described people, places, and events from the fantasy world he claimed to visit while he was in the coma. That was not unusual." Faeber paused, collecting his thoughts.

"The startling part was the detail to which Brian painted the images," Faeber said with wonder. "He described everything in first person. Not just visual and audible imagery, but smells, tastes, and touches as well. He commented on the weather, comparing it to past times as if he had been a native of that realm." He paused. "But he referred to himself as 'an outsider,' 'a traveler' in that world."

"And this is unusual?" Lamb queried.

"I have never experienced a subject under hypnosis who provided such complete detail," Faeber replied. "Of course, Brian was a creative boy. According to his mother he had always been, so I discounted the level of detail to his artistic nature."

"But something happened to change your opinion?" Liv said with anticipation.

"Yes," Faeber replied distantly. He opened the second notebook and withdrew some pieces of paper. "Under hypnosis, Brian drew the symbols on these pages, which he had said was the common script of his fantasy world." He put all but one of the sheets on the desk and slid them over. Strange characters were written vertically down the page in five columns.

"I could not identify the characters," Faeber continued, "They are arranged in columns, as are several east Asian written forms, but they are not similar to anything written in those languages."

"Most curious," Lamb agreed. "Dr. Rykov is an anthropologist. She might be able to make more sense of this."

"He drew the symbols on this page during our last session while under hypnosis."

Liv leaned forward to see the sheet, but Faeber kept the written side from them.

"Why is that one special?" Liv asked.

"Because while he was writing it, he brought himself out of the hypnosis!" Faeber paused. "I have not encountered, either personally or in the notes of my profession colleagues, a case where a subject brought themselves out from under hypnosis." Lamb nodded.

"But that was not startling part," Faeber said. "The startling part was that he started translating the characters into English while under hypnosis." He laid the sheet on the desk and turned it to face his guests, "And finished translating it after he had awakened!" Lamb and Liv both gasped. Lamb picked up the page and examined it more closely.

"And you will notice from how Brian translated it, that the message appears to flow from the center outward, with the columns alternating first to the right, then to the left, then the next on the right, and then the next on the left."

"That's weird," Liv said. But Lamb was more disturbed about the message he had written.

The mad wizard Gho-Bazh seeks to conquer the waking world to save mankind from Utgarda of the Bloody Trunk the demon-god messenger of chaos. But their war will destroy both worlds.

"In spite of the consistency of his stories under hypnosis," Faeber said with both relief and puzzlement, "I had hypothesized that these were all products of Brian's subconscious. But if that were the case, the imagery would not transfer with him from the unconscious to the conscious state. And to revive himself in the act of translating from one language to another that use different alphabets requires a high level of mental resources, some of which are believed by my learned peers to be dormant in either the conscious or the unconscious state."

"Why are you telling us this, Dr. Faeber?" Lamb asked.

"You've been sitting on this stuff for almost ten years," Liv added. "Why open up now?"

"When he was brought in here," Faeber replied, "Major Ganon only said two things in his semi-conscious state: that he needed to 'save Nygof from Gho-Bazh' and 'where is Anna?' Once he regained consciousness and I started assessing him, I realized that he was speaking of people and places that Brian had described during hypnosis."

"Ganon told us," Lamb said, "that he was a 'traveler' to the other realm, and that travelers could get there either voluntarily or involuntarily. Voluntary travelers knew who they were in both places, while involuntary ones only knew one persona. He claims that Gho-Bazh returned him to this world involuntarily, which is why he does not know who he is here."

"And how does he know the Gho-Bazh?"

Lamb and Liv exchanged glances. Lamb sighed again.

"Because he led Anna, Liv, and I on an expedition to rescue Brian from him." Faeber adopted an incredulous expression. "What's more," Lamb continued, "Brian drew pictures of this expedition that clearly show the four of us, as well as another acquaintance that Anna and I only met a few weeks ago." He paused, realizing how crazy that sounded. Then his eyes lit up. "Do you have Ganon's belongings?"

"I can get them," Faeber replied. "Why?"

"When we last met, he had evidence that will support our story," Lamb replied. "A drawing on canvas of five people."

"I am intrigued," Faeber said as he stood. "Wait here and I will get his things." Faeber left the office, closing the door behind him.

"Do you think he believes us?" Liv asked when she heard his footsteps walking away.

"His story is a strange as ours," Lamb replied, "and they kind of fit together. I just wish we had his sketchbook."

Faeber returned a few minutes later. He carried a wood box that was latched shut with a padlock. He placed the box on his desk, and opened the lock with a key on a ring he pulled from his pocket. Lamb stood to examine the contents, but Faeber put up a hand to stop him.

"The rules say that only I can remove things from this box." When Faeber pulled out Ganon's new suit, Lamb reached in, pulled out the scrap of canvas, and placed it on the table. Lamb pointed to his image.

"That is clearly me," he said, "who Ganon refers to as Nab. This is Liv here," he pointed to her image, "also known as Sif. This is Anna Rykov," he said pointing to that figure. "She is identifiable by the scars on her face." He pointed them out. "He calls her Nygof."

"And I can see that that is Ganon," Faeber added, indicating Ganon's figure. "Where did he get this?"

"On the other side," Liv said emphatically. "What's more, Anna has Brian's sketchbook with the original image."

"And did I mention that Brian made those drawings ten years ago?" Lamb added, "and none of us have ever met him."

Faeber blinked and sat in his chair again. He glanced from Lamb to Liv to the ceiling and back several times. Then he nodded confidently.

"I am convinced," he said. "I will release Major Ganon into your custody, Dr. Lamb."

"His name is actually Carver," Lamb corrected. "Major Preston Carver." Faeber nodded.

"I see," Faeber said, writing the name on a pad on his desktop. "The paperwork and authorization will take some time. I will go see to it."

◆

The Cavalier Club was a private gentlemen's club. O'Malley arrived shortly before the end of the business day, and his priestly garments were noticed by the passersby who saw him walk up to the twin red, leather doors. A large, grim-faced man in a grey suit stood outside the door. He stuck his hand up as O'Malley approached the door.

"Sorry, Father," the doorman said. "Members only."

"Tell Mr. Elder that I have come about this," O'Malley directed and pulled the letter from his pocket. He handed it to the doorman. The large man knocked on the door and a peephole slid open. The man put the paper through the hole.

"Wait here," a voice said from inside, and the peephole hatch closed.

Chapter 23

July 13, 1929

"Tell us what happened," Lamb said.

"Faeber's girl wouldn't let us talk to him," Ganon said, "so we left and headed back to the hotel. Traffic was heavy, so we got out and walked the last couple of blocks. We were almost there when that Gulden fellow appears out of nowhere."

"I don't like that guy," Lamb said. "It's like there's something at the edge of my memory about him that I just can't recall."

"Well," Ganon continued, "it doesn't get any better. He started hassling Anna to have dinner with him and talk about the case. Said he wanted to compare notes. She agreed since he was so persistent, so I begged off, but I followed them. They went to this restaurant on 43rd Street, and something didn't seem right."

"What was it?" Liv asked, engrossed in the tale.

"There were these two guys in overcoats and hats standing in the shadows at the other end of the block," Ganon said. "Gulden saw them," he paused for effect, "and then made the Sign of Utgarda at them! And they signed it back!" He stared at them with his mouth agape. "Well I knew something was amiss, so I went around to the back, and there were three big cars there, and more guys in overcoats."

"And then what happened?" Lamb asked with urgency.

"Well, those guys were all just standing around smoking," Ganon continued, "so I pretended to be drunk and wandered past them. They didn't seem to take notice of me. Just as I got to the back door, a guy came out with some trash, and I sneaked in past them all into the kitchen. I made for the dining room and found Anna pointing her gun at Gulden. There was a bunch of mob types at the table right behind her, and one of them shouted 'GUN' just as the two from out front came through the door and started shooting up the place."

"Is that when you got hurt?" Liv asked.

"No," Ganon said, shaking his head for a moment until some dizziness took over and he collapsed into her lap. He rose slowly with her help. "As soon as I saw the gunmen, I ran in there with my Elder Sign out and grabbed Anna. They mowed down the mobsters, but they were shooting at Anna." He paused for emphasis.

"How did you get away?" Lamb asked.

"The Elder Sign deflected the bullets," Ganon said, "and I pulled her into the kitchen and out the back door. That's when some goon sucker-punched me and knocked me out. I was awakened by some cops. The cars were gone, and so was Anna."

"Do you know how long you were unconscious?" Lamb probed.

"Don't think it was too long. The cops found me when they were first checking out the alley and sent me to the hospital. Before I know it, they got me locked up in the mental ward."

"Two men with machine guns shooting up a restaurant is more than we can handle," Lamb said. "If you're right, and the scene in the restaurant was to cover up an attack on Anna, we need to find her."

"Whoever they are," Liv said, "they're organized."

"That's right," Ganon agreed. "They signaled each other with the sign of Utgarda." He mimed the gesture quickly and looked around in case something was summoned. Lamb noticed the gesture and remembered something.

"Do that again," he demanded. Ganon shook his head.

"I don't want to risk calling something down on us," he said defensively.

"Draw it then," Liv said, handing Ganon a pad and pencil. Ganon drew the symbol.

"I've seen that before," Lamb said, suddenly, searching through the debris until he found yesterday's newspaper. He flipped the pages to the article about Brian Teplow and handed the page to Ganon. "I knew it!"

He pointed to the ad for the Church of Cosmic Understanding. Ganon's eyes widened. It was almost identical to what he had drawn. Lamb showed the article to Liv.

"It looks like they're having a gathering there tonight," Liv noted. "They're probably a small group, so if they want to recruit members, all the current members will probably be there."

"Then that's where we'll find Anna!" Lamb exclaimed.

◆

The room became indistinct as Anna succumbed to whatever she was been injected with. The others had left her alone in the darkened room again. Anna noticed a dim light around the door to the wardrobe. Once her attention was captured, the light increased until the room was bathed in an eerie, red hue as the spyhole in the wardrobe slid open. The face of the man inside was now made up in a theatrically evil-looking glare that seemed to bore through her.

She was in the column-lined courtyard of an east-Asian-style palace. Her neck, wrists, and ankles were tied to a cross beam with rough rope that bit into her skin.. Harry was similarly bound on her right, and the Lee woman was trussed up on her left. They wore the clothing from the drawing. Before them was arrayed a line of the horned beings from the subway, the Pointees. They held ornately-carved sticks with metallic veins running through them that glinted in the malevolent red sun. At the end of each, pointed toward them, were large crystals.

The man from the wardrobe now stood to one side of the horned beings. His evil face was crowned by a conical red hat that matched the red robes covering his tall, thin frame. He also held a crystal-tipped staff. Ganon was wearing the clothing he had on in the drawing, and was on his knees at the feet of the man.. His wrists were bound to a heavy yoke around his neck. He was bruised and bloody.

"*Throd gotha ngilyaa* Ganon *s'uhn gotha, lw'nafhyar ep naflmg ehye*," the man in the red robes said. "*H'ilyaa ilyaa uh'e Sif ee nilgh'ri, n'gha* brought me Nygof and Nab." Anna felt a warm, dry breeze on her face. Some of his words became clear to her.

"*Nabug 'fhalma* believe *uln gothaoth ron*," Ganon shouted, "*f'kadishtu* Gho-Bazh *ebunma* no choice." The nearest Pointee struck him with the base of its staff, and Ganon fell prone, his face hitting the ground with an audible crunch from the weight of the yoke behind it. The heat of the sun and surrounding stone increased, and Anna started to sweat.

"You seek *phlegethog ilyaa shogg*, Utgarda *k'yarnak* his conquest, *vulgtm wgah'n*," the robed man continued, "but this cannot be allowed!" Sweat flowed into Anna's eyes. He pointed the crystal of his staff toward Anna. A bright light shot forth from the Pointee crystals and engulfed her vision.

When her vision returned, Rose was laughing from the doorway. Anna's heart was pounded and her throat was sore. She had been screaming. The light was on. She looked at the wardrobe. The spyhole was closed, and there was no sound from within.

The dominatrix walked up and cupped Anna's chin roughly, and prodded her neck and wrists beneath the metal cuffs. Anna winced and noticed what appeared to be rough rope burns on her wrists, and realized that her neck was equally sensitive where it rubbed against the collar around her neck.

"I didn't make those," Rose said, annoyed. She looked at Anna. "I don't even use rope," she added to Anna conversationally. "My customers don't want any lasting marks!"

Rose looked at Anna and shook her head. Then, she stood and opened the peephole in the cabinet. The man within was unconscious. She flicked his nose with her finger and his eyes opened with surprise. She grinned, her annoyance apparently gone, and left the room.

◆

"Your new rooms are ready, Dr. Lamb," the hostess said, summoning a bellman to assist with the bundles he, Liv, and Ganon had purchased. "We found two adjacent rooms on the 11th floor for you," she continued. "Not as spacious as the suite, but your belongings have been moved to them. Here are the keys. The gentlemen are in room 1135 and Dr. Rykov is in 1137."

"Thank you," Lamb said to the hostess as the bellman relieved Liv of several small bundles. When he moved on to Lamb, the doctor handed him a covered golf bag, but insisted on keeping the other long bundle that he carried. The bellman complied, moving on to place Ganon's packages on the cart with the others.

The hostess turned to return to the desk and nearly walked into Kirby, who nodded to her with a smile and watched her walk away before he turned back to the three.

"Been shopping?" he asked sarcastically. "I gather you located Dr. Rykov."

"We know where she will be tonight," Lamb replied.

"If you'll excuse us," Liv added with a smile, "we need to prepare for this evening."

"Of course," Kirby said with a "better-I-don't-know" look. "I hope that your evening activities are pleasant." Lamb nodded and smiled. As they started toward the elevator, he added for all to hear, "Good hunting!"

Lamb did not visibly react, but he wondered if the detective had conjectured what they were up to. He hurried to the open elevator and joined the others. He could see that Liv was distressed by the comment.

When the doors closed, Ganon said, "That's a strange farewell."

Not wanting to speak frankly in front of the elevator operator or the bellman, Lamb replied, "it was a queer thing to say." He turned to the bellman. "Does Mr. Kirby often speak in tongues?"

"Oh, no, sir," the bellman said. "I overheard him earlier speaking with a police officer about the break-in to your suite. He's been in an odd mood since then."

"He's been up and down all day," the elevator operator added. "That kind of thing is bad for the hotel's reputation. He's worried about the safety of the guests. Especially as whoever done it didn't have to break in." The bell rang. "Eleventh floor," he said and pulled the lever to open the doors.

After they exited the elevator, the bellman led them to the rooms. He was reluctant to give Liv the key to Anna's room, but Lamb nodded his approval and took the key to the other room. They brought all the parcels into Lamb's room. The bellman waited impatiently until Liv gave him a quarter. His smile bloomed. He tipped his hat at her and left with the cart, closing the door behind him. Ganon listened at the door until he heard the elevator close.

"Lock the door," Lamb said in a serious tone, unwrapping the two shotguns and the Thompson submachine gun in his long bundle, "and let's get ready."

"Do you know how to use that?" Liv asked sarcastically as she opened another bundle to reveal four, round, drum magazines for the Thompson.

"How hard can it be?" Lamb replied, "Not likely that the regular folks will be armed, but those that are going to have these."

"So, let's run through the plan again," she stated with reservations.

"The 'conclave' at the Church of Cosmic Understanding starts at 8:00," Lamb said. "Sunset is at 8:34 tonight. We wait until after dark and then sneak in during the proceeding when the attendees are distracted. If things go as Ganon suggested, even the guards are going to be involved in whatever ritual they have planned."

"And we're going to carry shotguns and a machinegun in that golf bag?" Liv shook her head.

"Yes, and also Ganon's saber," Lamb replied, ignoring Liv's meaning altogether. "Once we're at the site and have concealed ourselves, we'll break out the guns."

"You need someone to get inside and look around before the attack," Liv said. "You two are known. I could get in there and eyeball the place so you have a better idea of what we'll need."

"Intelligence gathering is not something to take lightly," Lamb said. "Once you're in there, they might not let you out again."

"Then I'll scream," she said with irritation, "and you can rush in, guns ablazin'." She put her hands to her hips and glared at the two. "I'm more than capable of taking care of myself. I did just fine before you two came along."

"It would be smart to know the lay of the land," Ganon said. "If she can get in and look around, that'll be a big help."

"And that's why I brought this," Liv added, pulling a well-used Colt Model 1908 Vest Pocket pistol from a waistband holster under her jacket. She expertly extracted the six shot magazine, verified that it was full, and slapped it into place. "Satisfied?"

"If you're sure about this," Lamb said sheepishly. Liv gave him a stern look.

"OK then," Ganon said, oblivious to the tension between the other two. "Liv'll check out the surroundings and tell us what she sees. If we hear from her before she comes back, we'll bust in and start shooting." He grinned in anticipation.

"Good," Liv said, sliding the pistol back into her holster. She checked her wristwatch. "It's almost 5:00. Let's get this gear stowed and grab some dinner before we enter the lion's den."

Chapter 24

July 13, 1929

O'Malley waited at the door under the watchful gaze of the enormous doorman for a few minutes before the front door to the Cavalier Club opened and a smaller, but no less menacing man in a brown suit gestured for him to enter. In the foyer of the club there was a cloak room to one side.

"If you don't mind, Father," the man said, "please leave your bag with Pepper here." He indicated a pretty blonde wearing a sleeveless white shirt and a bow tie who smiled shyly at O'Malley when he glanced her way. When O'Malley hesitated, the man added, "unless it is relevant to your meeting, in which case I'll have to look through it."

"Very well," O'Malley said with a shrug, and handed the case to the girl. She handed him a ticket and he nodded with a smile.

Immediately before them, the wide double doors to the club itself were closed, but the small man opened a door opposite the cloak room, revealing a hallway that turned immediately to the left.

"Mr. Elder will see you in his office, Father," the man said. "Please follow me." He turned and led the priest down the hallway, which continued down the length of the building. They stopped at the first door and the man knocked.

"I'll take it from here, Louie," a large man in a grey suit said after emerging from another room down the hall. O'Malley noticed that the rest of the doors in the corridor had red lights next to them. Some were on and others were not. The man had emerged from the third door down, whose light was on. Another large man emerged from the room a moment later.

"I'm Mickey Elder, Father," the first man said, holding out his hand. O'Malley took it.

"Father Sean O'Malley," O'Malley replied, shaking the hand. Elder opened the door and guided O'Malley into the office.

"Please take a seat," Elder said as he walked around the desk and sat in his own chair. The other man entered the room and closed the door behind him. O'Malley glanced at the man and then took the offered chair. "Now, what can I do for you, Father?"

"I am here on behalf of Woody Frank," O'Malley said. Elder glanced at his colleague and raised his eyebrows.

"I'm sorry, Father," Elder said quickly, "but Woody made a deal, and his payment is long overdue."

"And that is why you sent him this note," O'Malley said in his best 'reproachful priest' tone. He handed the paper to Elder, who glanced at it and set it aside.

"That is correct," Elder replied calmly. "Woody agreed to the terms and has failed to meet them. It is now within my rights to collect."

"You won't be getting anything from Mr. Frank," O'Malley said. When he noted anger rising in Elder's face, he added, "He's dead." Elder's expression changed to surprise.

"What do you mean, he's dead?"

"I just came from his apartment where I found a man searching it. When he saw me," O'Malley paused for a moment and sanitized the story, "he attacked me and we fought." He indicated the holes in his cassock. "He got the better of me and escaped."

"What happened to Frank?"

"He was tied to the chair and had been cut many times. It appeared that he had bled to death."

Elder closed his eyes leaned into his steepled his fingers. He appeared to be upset. He took several deep breaths, laid his hands on the table, and opened his eyes to look at the priest.

"What brings you to me, Father?" Elder said in a quiet, calm tone.

"I went to see Mr. Frank because my colleagues have come to New York looking for Brian Teplow, the spirit medium who has gone missing. They were going to meet my ship when it docked this morning, but they did not show up. I was told that they had gone to see Mr. Frank. I went to his office and it had been ransacked. At the request of his secretary, I went to Mr. Frank apartment. I killed my attacker, but I found that note attached to a stack of bills from the Oak Valley Sanitarium." He handed the invoice to Elder. "I think that you are somehow involved in his disappearance, and may know where my colleagues are."

"But you don't think I had Woody killed?" Elder asked curiously.

"No," O'Malley replied. "The man who attacked me was…" he searched for the right words, "He was savage, desperate." He glanced to the man at the door. "I don't think you would employ such a man, and killing Frank would not get you your money."

"Who was supposed to meet you at the docks?" Elder asked, deliberately changing the subject.

"Some colleagues from Reister University," O'Malley replied with reservation. "Dr. Anna Rykov and Dr. Harold Lamb." The man at the door made an unintelligible sound, but Elder spoke first.

"Dr. Rykov has been my guest," Elder replied, gesturing with his head to the man at the door, who quietly left the room. "I've never heard of this Dr. Lamb."

"Is she here now?" O'Malley said anxiously. "How did you come to meet her?"

"Dr. Rykov witnessed uh, an incident, last night. My associates brought her here to tell me what happened."

◆

Liv approached the entrance to the Church of Cosmic Understanding, which inhabited an old stone church on East 10th Street mid-way between Third and Fourth Avenues. The structure had a stately, if worn, appearance. Men and women dressed in rust-colored monk's habits greeted a modest crowd gathered outside the front doors. Liv noticed that most of them were young women.

She left Lamb, Ganon, and their golf bag at the corner of Fourth and 10th after the three had done a casual stroll around the block. The single-story church was smaller than its five story neighbors. On one side, a small, ill-kept cemetery ran the length of the building faced by a low stone wall. There was an alley that disappeared around to the right between the neighboring building and the one behind the church. There was a narrow space barely wide enough for a person to enter between the church and the building on the other side that went all the way to East 9th Street. About halfway down the gap was a side door to the church.

Liv smiled as she approached a young, robed woman with stylishly-plaited hair outside the front door.

"Are you here for the conclave?" the woman asked politely.

"Yes," Liv replied. "I'm curious about the Church of Cosmic Understanding." She moved closer and said conspiratorially, "This isn't some sort of confidence act or flim-flam, is it?"

"No," the woman said with a knowing grim. "The Church of Cosmic Understanding is very real and has a long and storied tradition. I'm sure you will find the conclave most interesting." She gestured toward the door. "Please come in."

Liv looked about and noted some other people entering. "All right," she said, and followed the others.

Once inside the doors, Liv discovered that the men and women were being segregated. Ahead of them on the other side of the foyer, the women were sent through a door to the left, and the men through one to the right. Some of the people, couples mostly, decided not to separate and instead were politely directed to a door on the men's side, which Liv noted led to a stairway downward.

She followed the other women through the indicated door and down a long hallway, which she guessed ran the length of the church and ended in a descending stairway that curved to the right out of view. Something made Liv uncomfortable, and she turned to exit, but the column of women behind her blocked her path. Liv she tried to maneuver around the woman in her way, but the corridor was too narrow to pass.

"Please keep moving forward," a large, robed woman just inside the door said. "There are other people waiting to get in." Liv tried to protest, but the press of the others pushed her forward, and she reluctantly turned and continued. As she rounded the corner and went down the steps, she and several of the other ladies gasped at the dinginess of the stairwell and the musty smell, which increased as they descended further.

Liv lost count of the number of steps, but about halfway down, the column stopped. The stairwell was barely illuminated by lamps set in niches along the walls roughly every five steps. Liv had counted ten lamps so far and could see the light from several more to come.

"This is quite exciting, isn't it?" the fashionably-dressed brunette in front of Liv said with amusement. "I've been to several of these things…"

"So you know what happens here?" Liv interrupted. The woman shook her head.

"I haven't been here before," the woman said, "but I've been to other things like this. All very mysterious. It's either an exclusive speakeasy or a sex club." From her expression, Liv noted that neither prospect bothered the woman. Liv clutched her purse more tightly. Her confidant noted Liv's uneasiness. "Relax," she said with a friendly grin, "it'll be fun!"

◆

Rose stood in front of the open peephole in the cabinet and made faces at its inhabitant. The man made muted sounds that might have been laughter. Anna was surprised that the man was still alive. He had been in there since before she had arrived, and Anna had not once seen the man be given food or water. Rose turned and noticed her concern.

"Doesn't he need food, or at least water?" Anna asked. Rose gave her an expression of mock concern.

"He'll be fine," she said. "He was out while you were under." Rose smiled maniacally. Anna's mind raced. She noted a bitter, dry taste in her mouth, and suddenly her throat was dry as well. Her stomach rumbled. Rose giggled at Anna's expressions of discomfort and anxiety. Suddenly, the door opened and Louie entered.

"The boss wants her in the office," he said to Rose. The dominatrix's mirth faded. "The priest's been asking about her. The boss said she was here."

"Looks like your date is here," Rose said with a shrug. "Better get you cleaned up." With that, she left the room.

"Get me out of this chair," Anna demanded. The man shrugged.

"I don't know how," he said, "and if I do it wrong you might get hurt." Rose returned with a wet cloth and straddled Anna's lap.

"The last time they tried to mess with my stuff," she said, rubbing Anna's face roughly with the cloth, "the poor guy suffocated." Rose leaned forward, smothering Anna's face between her breasts, and Anna felt a slight construction on her neck, followed by an easing of the restriction as Rose manipulated something behind the headrest. Then she sat back and grinned malignly again.

"Snap to it!" Louie said. "The boss is waiting."

Rose scowled as she slowly stood and stepped behind the chair. There was a click, and the collar snapped open. Anna glared at the woman as she stepped back around and released first Anna's legs, and then her wrists. Once free, Anna leapt to her feet and punched Rose in the face. The dominatrix fell to the floor, blood flowing from her nose.

"I like her," Rose said with a wide smile.

Anna smiled back sarcastically and stepped toward the door. The man in the cabinet started making muffled sounds of laughter. Rose stood, slapped the peephole door shut, and flipped the switch. The man's laughter turned to sounds of torment as Anna went in the direction her escort indicated.

Lamb and Ganon waited on the corner. It had been almost fifteen minutes since Liv entered the church, and they were sweating in the thick, leather overcoats they had worn for protection. The plan had been for her to take a look inside and come right back, but it was starting to get dark, and there had been no sign of her.

"I don't like it," Lamb said, dropping the golf bag to the ground. Ganon winced and wrapped his arms around his head as the bag impacted with the concrete.

"Careful with that," Ganon said. "Don't forget what's in there!" Lamb sighed.

"We should get inside," Lamb said grimly and started unzipping the cover of the golf bag. Ganon put his hand on Lamb's.

"Too soon," Ganon replied. "We go in now and she'll be blown for sure." He glanced from Lamb to the entrance and back. "She'll send us a signal of some kind," he added confidently. "She's not going to let you down."

"We should at least get ready," Lamb said with reluctance. He scanned the scene across the street. The crowd had been admitted, and only three of the robed figures stood in front of the building. From their demeanor, they appeared to be more sentries that a welcoming committee. He picked up the golf bag again and the two started down the sidewalk toward 3rd Street, which afforded a view of the cemetery side of the church.

"There's no lights on in the sanctuary," Lamb noted.

"Maybe they do things by candlelight," Ganon replied, "though it is a rather dark in there." He prodded Lamb forward when he noticed one of the robed figures looking their way, and they walked casually to the corner and turned toward 11th Street.

"Do you think he marked us?" Lamb asked.

"Well there aren't too many folks walking around with big cases over their shoulders." Lamb nodded grimly. The golf bag had been an inspired idea to carry their weapons in, but it was rather conspicuous now that the sun was down.

"Let's get to the alley," Lamb said and stepped to cross Fourth Avenue. Ganon followed and they doubled back on the other side of the street. Once across 10th Street, they made their way into the alley that ran behind the building next to the church. From the shadows, they could see that the alley ran all the way to the building on the far side of the church. They could see a rear entrance to the church that led down a short flight of steps to the basement. There were two robed figures outside this entrance, which was illuminated with a burning torch mounted on either side.

As they huddled there, a door in the building across the alley opened from inside and a line of people in similar robes, their hoods up and their hands hidden in the sleeves of their robes, stepped out of the new doorway, crossed the alley, and entered the church. After the last one entered, the two at the door looked both ways down the alley before taking the torches from the sconces, stepping inside the door, and closing it behind them.

"I don't like the look of this," Ganon said. Lamb unzipped the golf bag. He removed the Thompson and a drum magazine and handed them to Ganon. Then he took a shotgun and a box of shotgun shells from the bag and started loading his weapon.

"I think it's time to rescue the damsel in distress," the doctor said, pumping the shotgun. "Let's go."

Chapter 25

July 13, 1929

Louie led Anna down the corridor, followed by Rose. Anna scowled as she rubbed her wrists. She was taken to the last door, which was open, to reveal a nicely-furnished office where the boss was seated behind a large desk, and Sean O'Malley was sitting across from him.

The priest rose as Anna entered. A wave of relief came over her as she ran up and embraced him. After a moment, Sean separated them with his hands on her shoulders and looked at her. He gasped when he saw the imprint on her chest and then the abrasions on her neck and wrists. Rose looked away.

"Are you alright?" O'Malley asked with concern, glaring at Elder. .

"She's fine," Elder said with a wave of his hand. "We just had a friendly conversation."

Anna was about to object when the man who took the sketchbook from Elder appeared, holding a newspaper folded open to a certain page. Rose took it from him and looked at the page before walking up to Anna.

"That's the ad I was talking about," Rose said, holding the folded newspaper next to Anna's chest. The design was the same. Anna stared at each man individually before buttoning up her blouse.

"How are you affiliated with this Church of Cosmic Understanding?" Elder asked, his interest visibly growing.

"My colleagues and I were tasked with stopping it," Anna replied. "I think that the attack was meant for me. That is why Gulden took me to that particular restaurant. Your associates were there to conceal the shooters' true target."

"So you're saying that this Church of Cosmic Understanding was after you?" the seated man said excitedly, "and Wendell was there to cover it up." He looked to Rose and Louie, then back to Anna. "Why should I believe you?"

Anna pulled Brian Teplow's sketchbook from her purse, put it on the desk, and flipped to the page with the drawing of the group. O'Malley glanced at the image, and then to Anna with a start. Anna ignored him.

"Those five people are central to Brian Teplow's visions. You can see that I have the scars in that drawing that I did not have in the previous one." She flipped between the two pages for comparison. "How could he have placed them so accurately?" she continued. "The other people in the photo are my colleagues. None of them knew Brian Teplow when those drawings were made ten years ago."

"That's the guy that pulled her out of the restaurant," Louie said, pointing to the image of Ganon.

"Yes it is," she said coolly. "He was one of the people who met Gulden for the first time this morning and had a bad feeling about him. When Gulden showed up on the street,

Ganon excused himself and followed us. He rescued me from the gunfight."

"How long have you known him?" Elder asked.

"I met him for the first time yesterday," Anna replied, "but he believes he knows me from the events in the drawings that follow." Elder flipped through the subsequent pages. When he reached the last one, he looked for more.

"Why does it stop?"

"According to my colleague, that was when we were captured by the tentacled entity's enemy."

"And why would his enemy capture you if you were tasked to defeat this tentacle thing?"

"That I don't know," Anna replied, wincing as she attempted to shrug. "It has something to do with looking for Brian Teplow. In that story, Teplow was that man's prisoner, and we were hired to rescue him."

"So you were hired first to stop the tentacle thing," Elder summarized, "and then to free a prisoner from its enemy."

"I do not know anything about the rescue mission," Anna said, "but the drawings of my colleagues and I did occur and we started seeing visions of the other drawings before we even knew about that sketchbook."

Elder closed his eyes and rubbed his chin again as he had done before. When he opened his eyes again, his expression was one of anger.

"Take the boys and check out this church."

"Right, boss," Louie replied automatically.

"If you are going to the Church of Cosmic Understanding," Anna said with urgency, "you may need my help." Elder looked at her skeptically. "I know what they are capable of, and I know how to fight the monsters."

"And I have some things in my valise that will be of assistance," O'Malley chimed in.

"You think there are monsters at the church?" Louie asked anxiously.

"Both human and non-human," Anna replied in a no-nonsense manner. Elder thought for a moment and nodded.

"Bring them," he said. "Rose will keep an eye on you, and if either of you cross me, you'll both be sorry."

◆

After watching the door to the building behind the church for a few minutes, Ganon moved quietly through the shadows toward the now darkened rear door of the church. He put his ear to the door, but could not hear through the thick metal barrier. There were no windows, and the only opening was the metal door.

Lamb scanned the wall of the church over the graveyard. There were windows into where the sanctuary should be, but there was about ten feet between the sunken floor of the graveyard and the lips of the sills. After focusing closely on the glass, he saw that there were painted silhouettes behind the glass. The windows had been covered over.

Lamb ran across the intervening space and joined Ganon at the door. Ganon readied the Thompson and nodded. Lamb pulled the handle, but the door did not move. It was locked.

"Looks like we're going to have to shoot the lock," Lamb said. "I don't see any other doors or windows."

"That's going to give us away," Ganon said, "but I don't see another option." He looked around. All was quiet. The only activity was on distant Fourth Avenue, beyond the graveyard and the neighboring building at the end of alley.

Lamb pointed the shotgun at the lock and looked to Ganon. Ganon nodded and Lamb pulled the trigger.

When Liv reached the bottom of the stairwell, she followed Helen, the friendly woman in front of her, through an open doorway. The robed woman at the entrance counted her as number twenty and stopped the line. Silently, a thick, oak door closed behind Liv.

The room Liv had entered was dark. Slowly, her eyes adjusted to the darkness and she noted some phosphorescent substance glowing faintly in patches on the walls. Despite the long line she had been in, the chamber was not crowded. The door monitor had counted to twenty, so perhaps the people in front of them had moved on before the current group had entered.

Then there was a grinding sound, and a heavy, stone door opened at the far side of the room. The chamber beyond was dimly lit by torches.

"Please enter the naos now," the robed woman said at the open portal.

The new arrivals passed through another stone doorway into a rectangular chamber with a sand-covered floor. The torches were stationed about ten feet apart in sconces mounted in the high walls at the lip of a gallery above where a couple dozen hooded, robed, and chanting figures looked down upon them.

"H'ee ehye naflwgah'n Utgarda nyth ee hafh'drn n'ghft lloig, phlegeth ron cn'ghft fhtagn phlegeth grah'nnyth, ftaghu ebunma lw'nafh s'uhn li'hee chtenffyar."

When Liv entered the space she noticed that the sand was sticky in places. She glanced downward and noticed dark splotches here and there. Then the stone door rumbled closed behind her.

Chapter 26

July 13, 1929

There was a roar as the Thompson spat bullets into the metal door. Lamb dove to the side as Ganon was initially thrown off by the weapon's recoil, but he recovered quickly and the door buckled. Lamb raised the shotgun and kicked in the door. There was a short, narrow passage through ten feet of concrete before another heavy door blocked the way. Beyond the portal, they could hear chanting.

"H'ee ehye naflwgah'n Utgarda nyth ee hafh'drn n'ghft lloig, phlegeth ron cn'ghft fhtagn phlegeth grah'nnyth, ftaghu ebunma lw'nafh s'uhn li'hee chtenffyar."

"They're calling to Utgarda," Ganon said emphatically and pointed the submachine gun at the door.

◆

As Liv stepped across the sandy surface, her surroundings became warm, hazy, and took on a reddish hue. Helen stepped on one of the dark splotches and her shoe stuck to it, coming off her foot when she attempted to free it. The robed figures above chanted ominously. In the torchlight, their eyes appeared to glow every now and then. Liv drew her pistol.

Suddenly, a leathery tentacle erupted from the sandy floor and wrapped around a brunette wearing a short flapper dress. Then, another one shot out and grabbed a buxom blonde. The brunette fainted and was pulled under the sand, but the blonde screamed and struggled. As she watched in horror, Liv saw the tentacle squeeze tighter until the woman's torso burst. Entrails splattered across the sunken chamber, spraying other women, who started screaming and running in all directions.

A short woman wearing a tiara that sparkled like little explosions in the crimson light bumped into Liv and knocked her down onto her back. Then, another tentacle whipped out and the tiara landed in front of Liv as its owner's terrified face, her mouth agape as sand poured into it, will pulled under the sand . Liv tried to stand, but her jacket was stuck to the ground.

◆

Ganon fired a focused burst at the doorknob and it flew away. Lamb kicked open the door. The room beyond was dominated by an open space in the center. Evenly-spaced columns supported the ceiling, and robed, hooded figures peered down between them into the atrium below while chanting fanatically.

From their vantage point, Lamb and Ganon could not see what was happening, but when screaming erupted from below, they opened fired at the nearest chanters. A cloud of red mist rose as five of the cloaked figures pitched over the balcony.

◆

The sound of gunfire filled the air and Liv saw several of the robed people fall down into the sand. She struggled to rise, but her sleeves were coated with the sticky substance. More tentacles rose from beneath the sand to snatch up the panicking women and drag them below the surface.

Liv struggled out of the jacket and into a sitting position, but she was still holding her automatic, which got caught in the sleeve. Unwilling to release the weapon, she tugged until the lining tore and the hand and pistol were free. Then, a heavy weight struck her back and she was pushed forward, face down, into the sand where a strong, muscular appendage wrapped around her arms and torso. As Liv struggled against the constricting bands, she was lifted into an empty, reddish sky dotted with stars.

◆

"Like shooting fish in a barrel," Ganon shouted, smiling widely as the Thompson tore a swath through more of the cultists. Some of the robed figures dove for cover behind the columns and produced firearms of their own. They shot back while their brethren continued to chant. Lamb ducked behind the door they had entered through just before several shots struck it with dull thuds. Suddenly, the roar of the Thompson stopped as the last of the bullet casings tinkled to the floor.

◆

Liv was frozen with terror as the massive creature rose out of the sand. It was humanoid in shape with leathery, greenish-brown skin. The mass of long, blood-red tentacles that protruded from its face merged together into a massive trunk that now gripped her tightly. Two long, clawed arms emerged from below, and as the right hand rose up toward her, Liv saw a massive, malign eye in the center of the palm look her over from head to toe. Then, a narrow, sticky tongue snaked out from the end and licked her face.

Liv screamed. The coating of the tongue burned her flesh. She couldn't raise her arm to shoot the tongue, so she closed her eyes and fired her pistol repeatedly in the direction of the eye until there were no more bullets. There was a keening howl, and she felt herself whipping through the air as the trunk writhed chaotically. When she opened her eyes, greenish ooze flew from the punctured eye as the hand shook violently. An audible hiss arose from wherever the caustic ooze landed and it dissolved whatever it came into contact with.

◆

Several of the cultists grabbed long knives and rushed at Ganon. He dropped the Thompson and crouched to defend himself. The sound of metal sliding across the tiled floor distracted him for a moment, and a blade struck the inside of Ganon's left arm. Ganon was knocked back by the attacker's momentum, and hit the ground as Lamb's shotgun blast shredded the cultist.

Ganon ignored the wound and rolled to pick up the saber Lamb had slid on the ground to him. The sword was like an extension of his arm, and it sliced through the chest of the next attacker before piercing the throat of the one behind him.

Lamb continued to fire his shotgun to alternate sides of Ganon until it was empty. The cultists appeared to be taking cover. He ducked behind the door to reload.

Suddenly, he heard Liv scream, followed by an unearthly roar. Then, the tentacle-faced giant from Brian Teplow's sketchbook rose from the atrium, Liv struggling against the appendage wrapped around her, until it towered over them, the dark sun casting a blood-red pall over the temple and the barren, rocky landscape that now stretched out in all directions.

Three cars came to a screeching halt in front of the Church of Cosmic Understanding. They blocked traffic, but no one complained when Elder, Rose, Anna, and O'Malley, accompanied by six men armed with Thompson submachine guns stepped from the vehicles.

"What was that?" Mickey Elder cried when an unearthly roar erupted from within the building.

"We're too late," Rose said with an amused expression.

"That was Utgarda," Anna said stoically.

"Not necessarily," O'Malley replied, patting his valise.

"We need to get in there and stop it, "Anna shouted. "Give me my gun!" Rose shook her head until Elder nodded. Then, with a pout, she handed the pistol to Anna. Anna checked the magazine, chambered a round, and ran for the doors followed by O'Malley. The gangsters hesitated.

"You heard the lady," Elder shouted. "These are the punks that whacked Wendell! Let's go!" At once, the eight gunmen climbed the steps after Anna and the priest. There were three doors at the top.

"Split up," Elder ordered.

"No!" Anna shouted. "If we are divided, we will be overwhelmed." She examined the doors and selected the middle one. "Open this one!" One of the thugs fired a burst at the closure, and the ornate handles flew apart. Then he kicked in the door and charged inside.

◆

At the sight of their god, the hooded cultists transformed. Their cloaked forms hunched over into squatting positions. The cloaks morphed into scaly, greenish skin similar to that of the giant. Writhing tentacles sprouted from their faces. Their arms flattened out into wings, and talons sprouted from their feet. At once, the cultist creatures took flight. Some swooped down into the atrium. Others flew off at random, circling around the temple. Several leapt at Ganon.

Lamb peeked around the door and saw the flying monsters for the first time. He started shooting. The buckshot easily shredded the creatures, but the shotgun was quickly empty again.

Ganon was beset by three of the flying things. One of them hovered and lashed out with its claws at his face and chest while the other two took turns swooping past and raking his back. Ganon expertly slashed at the monsters, parrying claws and then turning to slice into the creatures as they flew past, but his thick coat was torn and his back was bloody.

◆

Liv struggled against the giant tentacle, but the grip was too tight. The pain was extreme. Her skin burned and her clothing smoked and disintegrated as the tongue continued to probe her head and shoulders. She had dropped the pistol when the constriction squeezed her to the point where she could barely breathe. The trunk continued to whip wildly in the blighted crimson sky, but Liv was too terrified to be sick. The thing roared again, its gigantic maw immediately below the base of the trunk, and Liv was deafened.

◆

The gangsters did not hesitate at the second door, which was down a short passage beyond the first. The lead gunman fired another burst and kicked in the door, stepping aside to allow the others to pass as he changed magazines.

Anna entered first, followed by O'Malley and Rose, and surveyed the scene as the gangsters fanned out behind them. It was utter chaos. The space beyond was not a room, but a colonnaded reproduction of a Roman-style temple. In the center was a pit surrounded by columns, but there was no pediment. Utgarda rose from the pit. One of his hands was spraying acidic fluid wildly as its arms passed harmlessly through the columns.

Smaller, winged creatures flew around, some swooping into the pit and emerging with shrieking women in their talons. Others menaced some figures at the opposite end of the temple.

"What are those things?" Elder asked in astonishment.

"Those are Utgarda's cultists," Anna said. "The advertisement was to collect sacrifices to summon him, and as a reward, they have been granted those forms."

Suddenly, a spray from Utgarda's hand struck across one of the gangsters. His gun was instantly split in two, and the rounds in the magazine cooked off in random directions when they came in contact with the acid. O'Malley knocked Anna to the ground as the shots flew past, and two of their group on the other side of Anna were struck and collapsed to the floor.

The man hit by the acidic spray screamed as his suit and the skin beneath melted away. Alerted by the noise, several of the flying monsters changed direction and closed on the new arrivals.

"You take care of the winged things," O'Malley shouted to Elder, who was still dumbstruck. "We'll handle Utgarda." Anna looked at O'Malley incredulously and crawled after the priest toward the lip of the pit. She turned at the sound of a slap, and saw Rose strike Elder's face a second time, and then push him behind a column as the flying monsters attacked.

"How do you propose to 'take care of Utgarda?'" Anna asked O'Malley as they looked over the lip of the atrium.

"The Order has provided me with some tools," O'Malley said, patting his valise. "In addition to the compounds we used in Wellersburg," he added, surveying the bloody scene below, "I also have some other devices that will be of assistance." As he looked about, he noticed that the walls of the church were becoming translucent.

◆

"I'm almost out of ammo," Lamb shouted to Ganon as he dropped the last of the shotgun shells into the magazine. There was another drum for the Thompson in the bag, but from his cover behind the now-battered metal door, he could see the weapon on the floor in the open about ten feet away.

Ganon continued to fight the flying minions, but had been backed into a corner of the room. He was using one of the columns as cover and slashing out with his saber to one side and then the other. The sleeves of his coat were shredded, and his arms, legs, and face were covered in blood.

The shotgun seemed to keep the creatures at bay. The spray of the pellets ripped through the things easily, so they avoided it. Instead, they attempted to strike at Lamb from multiple directions at once, but the door effectively shielded him from all but the front and top.

Lamb removed the last drum magazine from the golf bag. Then, he took a deep breath, pushed off the near wall on his back, and slid across the floor toward the Thompson, pumping and firing the shotgun repeatedly at the flying menaces.

◆

"H'ee ehye naflwgah'n Utgarda nyth ee hafh'drn n'ghft lloig, phlegeth ron cn'ghft fhtagn phlegeth grah'nnyth, ftaghu ebunma lw'nafh s'uhn li'hee chtenffyar."

"That speech sounds familiar," Anna said, hearing the chant. The gangsters' weapons roared as the swooping creatures dove and slashed at them. The bullets appeared to pierce the things, but did not appear to impair them much.

Something was not right, Anna thought. The giant's bulk should have filled the whole of the pit below, but somehow did not. And its sweeping arms should have knocked over the columns as they passed through them, but they didn't. Then, she noticed that the floor of the pit was covered with sand that seemed to match the sand surrounding the temple on that alien plain.

"Utgarda is not actually here yet," Anna proclaimed, attempting to be heard over the sounds of battle all around. "The cultists are attempting to transport the entire structure to Utgarda's realm, but the attack has weakened the ritual." She noted the few figures chanting. She turned back toward the gangsters and shouted "Shoot the ones chanting!"

The gunmen did not respond, continuing to fire blindly. Only two of the original five were still standing. But Elder and Rose, who had each collected a Thompson from their fallen companions, turned toward the remaining human cultists and fired. The chanting stopped abruptly.

◆

Utgarda roared and lashed out toward Rose and Elder with its claws, but they passed right through the pair. It struck out with its trunk, releasing Liv, who flew screaming over Anna and O'Malley and out into the desolate landscape.

When the trunk impacted with the column Elder hid behind, the pillar toppled over and fell into the pit. The tongue shot out from the blood-red appendage toward Elder.

Rose fired her weapon directly into Utgarda's face, and was rewarded with sprays of acid where the bullets struck. She laughed hysterically as she was hit in several places by the substance and her exposed skin started to bubble and melt. She turned and shot at the trunk, severing the end before her hands melted away and the weapon fell to the floor.

Elder leapt to the floor, avoiding the trunk, and slid to Rose's side. The acid was crawling across her face from the forehead down. She laughed maniacally as the rest of her face and then her neck burned away. Elder cradled Rose in his arms and wept.

◆

Lamb heard Liv scream and saw her fly away. When the chanting stopped, the solidity of the building returned. He had retrieved the Thompson and replaced the drum magazine. At the sight of Liv disappearing into the distance, Lamb surged with rage, firing the submachine gun at the back of the red-trunked giant's head.

Utgarda's head twisted convulsively, its trunk straight up, and it roared loud enough that the building shook. As it did so, the remaining flying creatures started circling Utgarda, blocking as many of the bullets as hit the giant.

In the meantime, O'Malley had been cowering behind one of the columns pulling the stoppers from many of the various vials that he had pulled from each of the three racks in the valise.

◆

Anna got Louie's attention, and the thug crawled toward her and O'Malley. Two of the henchmen remained, still firing their Thompsons at the flying creatures that now circled the giant.

When they reached the priest, O'Malley handed Anna one of the racks. He tried to hand one to Louie, but the gangster was watching Utgarda's trunk fly around to avoid the spraying acidic fluid. A sulfurous fog was rising as the surfaces it hit melted away. Anna slapped Louie several times across the face. The big man caught her hand reflexively after a few strikes, blinked several times and then accepted the rack Anna thrust at him.

"This will banish Utgarda to his home dimension," O'Malley yelled over the roar of the guns.

"We need to hit him where the bullets have struck him," Anna added. "Those are the only spots that are actually in this dimension." Louie looked blankly at each, and then nodded understanding.

"I will go around to the left," O'Malley said. "You go to the right," he said to Anna, "and you throw from here," he said to Louie.

"Hit him where he's been shot," Anna added once more as she ran off. O'Malley looked to Louie. The gangster nodded, and the priest sprinted to the other side of the pit.

◆

The sound of the machine guns died away as the ammunition ran out. All but a couple of the flying monsters had been destroyed, and the last two were perforated in many places.

"Now!" O'Malley shouted, and all three racks flew toward the giant. One rack exploded in the center of the giant's torso and another shattered against its head. Utgarda batted at the third vial, but it exploded on impact with the wounded hand.

There was another explosive roar that shook the building. This time, the columns started to crack and dust began to fall from the ceiling. There was a bright flash of reddish light, and Utgarda was gone. The sulfurous fog and reddish hue were gone and the temple was again enclosed within the structure of the church.

Anna continued around the perimeter of the room until she collided with Lamb. The doctor nearly fell into her arms, and they embraced. The loud rumbling from above abbreviated their reunion as the doctor picked up Anna and carried her through both of the rear doors into the alley. There was a loud crash, and the two were struck by a thick cloud of dust and debris as the walls and ceiling of the church collapsed.

Chapter 27

July 15, 1929

"My sweet Brian," Maureen Teplow cried when she saw Father O'Malley with Anna and Lamb at her front door. Anna caught her as she started to fall, Mrs. Teplow's tear-soaked face in her hands.

"Relax, Mrs. Teplow," Anna said, pulling her to her feet. "We believe we have found Brian and he is well." Mrs. Teplow lifted her head from her hands and kissed Anna's cheek.

"Bless you," she said, then stepped back. "Come inside!" Without waiting for her guests, the elderly woman walked into the living room and sat heavily on one of the sofas. Her face glowed with a wave of relief. Anna, Lamb, and O'Malley entered the house. O'Malley closed the door behind him before joining the others.

"This is Father Sean O'Malley," Anna said as she sat next to the woman, "He is a colleague of ours from the university."

"I apologize for the start," O'Malley said, taking a seat next to Lamb on the opposite sofa, "but we believe we have good news!"

◆

Following the collapse of the Church of Cosmic Understanding, Anna and Lamb found O'Malley, Elder, Louie and two of his gang in the front of the building. The marble structure had collapsed into an impenetrable pile of rubble in the atrium. At the sound of police sirens, Elder ushered them into one of the cars and drove off. His associates collected the other two cars and followed at speed.

"What the hell just happened?" Elder asked from behind the driver's seat.

"We just prevented the apocalypse," Lamb replied from the passenger seat. Anna and O'Malley were in the back seat of the sedan. He examined Anna's abrasions and rubbed some of the green fluid on her neck and wrists. She winced, but the marks immediately started to fade.

"That giant being was Utgarda, the god of the cultists," Anna said authoritatively. "They were trying to bring him to our dimension by offering the people in the pit as sacrifices."

"But our intervention quashed it," Lamb interjected.

"Yes," Anna continued. "When we interrupted their ritual, Utgarda was only partially in our dimension."

"And by transforming some of the cultists into those winged monsters to defend himself," O'Malley added, "he not only weakened the ritual, but instead started pulling the church…"

"Or rather the temple inside the church," Anna interrupted, "into its own dimension instead."

"Why?" Elder asked with curiosity.

"Utgarda's presence was stronger than the will of the remaining chanters," Anna replied.

"Kind of like when a piece of metal is placed between two magnets," Lamb added, "and one is stronger than the other."

"So," Elder concluded, "when they were all chanting, the cultists were stronger than the giant thing, but when they changed, it tilted the balance?"

"Exactly," Anna said.

"But how did you figure that out?" Lamb asked.

"When I was the prisoner of that woman," Anna scowled, "they injected me with something that they recovered from Peter Gulden's apartment."

"I'm sorry about that," Elder said sincerely.

Anna was not sympathetic. "That serum took me to the other dimension," Anna continued. "I didn't realize it at first, but I was slowly becoming aware of the surroundings and understanding the language that was being spoken."

"What did you see there?" Lamb asked, curiosity evident in his wide eyes.

"Our execution," Anna replied flatly. "At the hands of Gho-Bazh. A firing squad. You, Sif, and I were bound, facing a firing squad of those things from the subway. They had staves with crystals at one end. On Gho-Bazh's command, they fired."

"What happened next?" O'Malley asked with concern.

"I awoke," Anna continued. "I was still imprisoned in the chair, but I had the cuts from the ropes that had bound me." She pulled up her pants to reveal similar wounds on her ankles. "I supposed I was not sufficiently present in that dimension, so when they shot me, I returned to our world."

The car stopped in the alley behind the Cavalier Club. Elder stepped out and opened the door for Anna.

"You are all my guests," the gang boss said as the other cars stopped behind them. "Eat, drink, rest. Whatever you need." He opened the back door and Anna entered, heading to the room in which she had been imprisoned.

"The first thing is to release the man in that cabinet," Anna replied. But when she opened the door, there was no sign of the man who had been inside. In fact, the cabinet contained linens. And there was no peephole in the door or button on the side.

Anna looked about the room. All the implements of menace were gone. They were in a bedroom. She burst past Lamb and O'Malley and opened the other doors. All of the rooms were similarly furnished, two of which were occupied.

"Make yourselves comfortable," Elder said. "There is a bathroom in the club where you can clean up." He gestured toward the opposite end of the hallway. "I'll see to some nice steaks for you."

◆

"So Mr. Frank hired Elder and his gang to kidnap Brian and take him to a sanitarium upstate," Anna said, concluding her story.

"Why didn't the authorities find him there?" Mrs. Teplow asked.

"He was admitted under the name Daniel Meldon," Lamb replied.

"All you need to do is go there with proof that he is your son," O'Malley added, "and they will release him into your custody."

"Dr. Faeber at Bellevue has already agreed to resume his treatment of Brian," Lamb said.

"If he even needs treatment," Anna interjected. "Nothing that Brian has done warrants medical attention." Lamb looked at her incredulously. "To the public at large," she continued, "he is merely a celebrity who disappeared and has returned. A publicity stunt, perhaps."

"I don't think I want him in the public eye anymore," Mrs. Teplow said, shaking her head. "He's going to come home and stay here with me."

"Then he can publish those stories of his," Lamb said in a moment of inspiration.

"They were very well written," Anna agreed. "I'm sure that, given his celebrity, there will be interest in them."

"We'll see." Mrs. Teplow was visibly relieved, but suddenly seemed pale and weak. She swooned, but quickly recovered with a smile. Lamb came to her side and took her pulse.

"Excuse me," she said with embarrassment, "but this whole experience had been quite taxing."

"Is there someone who can look in on you?" Lamb asked. "You need to rest."

"But what about Brian?" Mrs. Teplow asked with panic in her voice."

"We will go to Oak Valley Sanitarium and retrieve him," Lamb replied. "All we need is a letter from you authorizing us to pick him up, and a letter from Dr. Faeber saying that he will continue the treatment."

"You've already done so much," Mrs. Teplow said feebly. "I couldn't impose on you further."

"It would be our pleasure," Anna said with a smile.

ABOUT THE AUTHOR

Joab Stieglitz was born and raised in Warren, New Jersey. He is an Application Consultant for a software company. He has also worked as a software trainer, a network engineer, a project manager, and a technical writer over his 30-year career. He lives in Alexandria, Virginia.

Joab is an avid tabletop RPG player and game master of horror, espionage, fantasy, and science fiction genres, including Savage Worlds (Mars, Deadlands, Agents of Oblivion, Apocalypse Prevention Inc, Herald: Tesla and Lovecraft, Thrilling Tales, and others), Call of Cthulhu, Lamentations of the Flame Princess, Pugmire, and Pathfinder.

Joab channeled his role-playing experiences in the Utgarda Series, which are pulp adventure novels with Lovecraftian influences set in the 1920's.

You can follow Joab on Twitter @JoabStieglitz, on Facebook, and on his blog: joabstieglitz.com.

JOAB STIEGLITZ

THE OLD MAN'S REQUEST

BOOK ONE OF THE UTGARDA SERIES

The Old Man's Request

Book One of the Utgarda Series

Fifty years ago, a group of college friends dabbled in the occult and released a malign presence on the world. Now, on his deathbed, the last of the students, now a trustee of Reister University enlists the aid of three newcomers to banish the thing they summoned.

Russian anthropologist Anna Rykov, doctor Harry Lamb, and Father Sean O'Malley are all indebted the ailing trustee for their positions. Together, they pursue the knowledge and resources needed to perform the ritual.

Hampered by the old man's greedy son, the wizened director of the university library, and a private investigator with a troubled past, can they perform the ritual and banish the entity?

The Old Man's Request is a pulp adventure set in the 1920s, and the first book in the Utgarda Series.

Available in paperback and ebook formats, and as an Audible audiobook

THE OTHER REALM

BOOK THREE OF
THE UTGARDA SERIES

JOAB STIEGLITZ

The Other Realm

Book Three of the Utgarda Series

Having discovered the location of Brian Teplow, Russian anthropologist Anna Rykov, doctor Harry Lamb, and Father Sean O'Malley travel to a secluded asylum to collect him.

But things are not so simple, and Anna must travel to the land of Teplow's imagination to rescue him, where she finds a different world from the one suggested in the Missing Medium's journals.

The Other Realm is a pulp adventure set in the 1920s, and the third book in the Utgarda Series.

Available in paperback and ebook formats, and as an Audible audiobook

THE HUNTER
IN THE
SHADOWS
BOOK ONE OF THE THULE TRILOGY
JOAB STIEGLITZ

The Hunter in the Shadows

Book One of the Thule Trilogy

After dreaming that her alter-dimensional sister Sobak was in danger, Anna Rykov is sent to Depression era Boston to find and kill the shape shifting alien who has captured her, and whose plans could bring about the extinction of all life on Earth

Anna is assisted by Cletus the hound and a homeless World War I veteran with skeletons in his own closet. However, Anna's inquiries catch the attention of J. Edgar Hoover, whose motives in this case are unknown.

The Hunter in the Shadows is a pulp adventure set in the 1930s, is the first book in the Thule Trilogy, and the fourth book in the Utgarda Series.

Available in paperback and ebook formats, and as an Audible audiobook

Made in the USA
Middletown, DE
12 September 2022